Astrocounselling

by Ross Prufrock

Published by New Generation Publishing in 2023

Copyright © Ross Prufrock 2023

First Edition

The author asserts the moral right under the Copyright, Designs and Patents Act 1988 to be identified as the author of this work.

All Rights reserved. No part of this publication may be reproduced, stored in a retrieval system or transmitted, in any form or by any means without the prior consent of the author, nor be otherwise circulated in any form of binding or cover other than that which it is published and without a similar condition being imposed on the subsequent purchaser.

ISBN   978-1-80369-726-0

www.newgeneration-publishing.com

Contents

INTRODUCTION 1

NATASHA 3

HANNAH 12

EMILY 21

GABRIELLE 30

ANNE 39

VENETIA 48

JANET 57

SALLY 66

DEBBIE 75

MEGAN 84

PAULA 92

REBECCA 101

INTRODUCTION

The purpose of this book is two-fold: to create with kindness and affection an honest portrait of twelve women and to link each of these portraits with a sign of the zodiac. It is a work of fiction. I have used the experience and knowledge I have from working as a counsellor to weave together these stories. I can vouch for the authenticity of the life experiences these women have had, but there has been a good deal of shuffling the pack of these experiences in order to produce an amalgam that gives, I hope, verisimilitude to the individuals I have created.

My experience both as a counsellor and a man have informed and underlie all these portraits. I have attempted to be kind and loving to all these people because that is the least all of us deserve. The majority of chapters are set in a counselling situation but this does not pretend to be a handbook on counselling. The counsellor, as I have portrayed him, is flawed in many ways – mainly because he is male. He tries and does his best, but, like everyone, is imperfect. *

In each portrait there is some material that links the individual with a particular sign of the zodiac. I envisaged it being fun for the reader to try to identify the zodiac energies traditionally associated with each sun sign. For a counsellor, though, it is important to focus on the reality of the person in front of you rather than to even begin to put someone in a box in accordance with a preconceived view of their zodiac energy**.

The first person protagonist in these stories is male. So there is a very real male gaze on these women, which might account for there being a good deal of focus on their sexual experiences. But there is nothing invented in what I have written about these experiences.

The main point, though, of having a slightly voyeuristic male counsellor was that the reader could guess what his sun sign might be. The reader is asked to submit her/his answers as to which sun sign goes with each individual – and then, for a tiebreak, to identify the counsellor's sun sign. These are portraits of women in real life situations – the breaking of the mother/child bond, the disaffection with a life of service/ an abusive relationship/rape/ the search for love, meaning and identity and so on. I hope they ring bells and send echoes of compassion towards all of them. Read about them, identify with them – and then have fun in apportioning the relevant zodiac energies! You can email bookshfp@yahoo.com to check your hunches.

* It might be argued that I have recorded enough examples of bad counselling practice that this little book could be used in counsellor training as a 'what-not-to-do' book! In my protagonist's defence I do believe that he complies with the positive values of counselling – listening, empathy, acceptance, compassion and judicious questioning. But this is not a book like Irvin D Yalom's *Love's Executioner* which gives much more detailed case histories and is certainly a boon to counsellor training.

** In fact I have kept to this maxim – being aware of the subject rather than the sun sign – throughout this book. So some sun signs are more difficult to determine than others. I suggest you begin with Emily and Anne and Venetia as, I think, they are the most obvious ones.

NATASHA

Natasha came to me late in her life – and late in mine for that matter. Basically she just wanted to be able to talk about a current problem which stemmed from her past. Aged 71 she accepted that it was a problem she could do little to solve, but there was so much going on inside her head and she had nowhere to unload it all. So she came to me. And it all poured out. I did suggest that it would be cheaper for her to write it all down, but she explained that she couldn't do that without arousing the interest of her husband. His interest had already quite recently been aroused by correspondence she had received from an old lover, and she had had to burn this correspondence. Her home and marriage did not provide her with any privacy, so writing was out of the question. Anyway she was an extravert person, liking making contact with people – which exacerbated the problem she had, the problem which was constantly buzzing around in her head and which she was desperate to release by talking about it.

It was in fact this old lover that was the problem. He was dying and had written to her wanting her to know how much he had loved her. Not only that but he had written two short stories about their time together and their shared intimacies, both enclosed in the package he had sent. The stories brought back such memories and she had devoured them and tingled with memory of all the love they had shared – and the love she was missing. She knew her husband, John, would not understand them and would – "quite rightly," Natasha added – perceive them as undermining their relationship. With much sadness she had had to burn the stories. She had written, though, to this old lover, assuring him that "I loved you too."

I picked her up on the "quite rightly", and she sighed and explained that she had retreated into a comfortable ordinariness since her marriage, her second one, to John.

He was a practical uneducated man who was content to be comfortable. Non-challenging, but devoted to her and not deserving of having his peace of mind disturbed by her ex-lover. Natasha herself had retired some ten years previously from a demanding job as PA to quite an important man in the city where her language skills had been invaluable. She was a quick thinker too; no one could say she was a deep thinker but she could think and adjust on her feet. All assets in her line of work. But once she had retired, suddenly the stimulus had gone from her life – which, at first, she enjoyed. She could relax. And then, when she realised that a kind of passive contentment was not enough for her (though it was for John as long as he could potter along doing the odd occasional job) she focused on her children and grandchildren as being the source of energy and fulfilment she needed. As her daughter and children lived in Germany and her son and children in France she got some stimulation from the travelling she did "but not quite enough." Though she hastened to add that, whatever her situation had been, she would always have made time for her children and grandchildren.

I wanted to move her onto talking about this lover who, apparently, was the source of her discontent, but Natasha wanted to explain that she and John did have a good deal of compatibility and there was one thing they happily did together, which was to work at one of the local Food Banks. It was run by the Methodist Church to which they both belonged and which gave then an underlying simple faith in God. "John is a good man. I just find him boring – and prematurely old. (He's my age.) I didn't fully realise this until Chris contacted me. I had received Christmas cards and birthday cards regularly from Chris over the years, but his recent profession of so much love and his stories have really shaken me."

Natasha's childhood history was grounded firmly in the Methodist Church where her parents, and theirs before them, were conscientious worshippers. She and John had first met there. But it was also the place where she had first met Chris. He was a teacher some ten or eleven years older than she was, and she had known him to say hello to from the age of eight. And then in Sixth Form College, studying A Level English Literature, he was suddenly her teacher – and, at first slowly and then blazingly quickly the dynamics of their relationship had changed. "We were familiar with each other from the outset. It felt good that I could easily talk with him about pretty well anything. And then came the College play."

It was *Twelfth Night* and Natasha played the servant Maria. Chris was directing. The cast had had a great time in rehearsal: "we all got on so well together. It was a great atmosphere." Before the dress rehearsal a cast photo was taken, and Natasha stood next to Chris and, without thinking, reached for and squeezed his hand. He squeezed back and "it felt like an electric current had passed between us." In her aroused excitement Natasha had gone over the top in her acting and Chris had had to tell her to tone it down. After the dress rehearsal Natasha had deliberately changed slowly and hung around waiting for Chris. The actor playing Andrew Aguecheek had taken an interminable time to pack his things and go, but finally there was only Chris and Natasha in the building. "We looked at each other. I was very nervous. But then he kissed me – tenderly at first, but I responded and we kissed and kissed passionately. It was just kissing, though."

It escalated. College was too risky a place, so they found a quiet place to meet after classes and sat together in the front seat of Chris's car and snogged and felt each other. Never in the back seat, though. That might have led to full intercourse, and they wanted their first time to have more dignity – and comfort – than in a cramped car. In fact their first time was not a success. Chris's wife had recently given birth to a baby boy (for whom Natasha got the job of baby sitter and the joy of being picked up and driven home by Chris on the occasions she sat) and one Saturday morning Chris's wife and child had driven to go shopping in a town twenty miles away. That was their opportunity. And it proved disastrous. They rushed upstairs to the marriage bed, could hardly wait to make love. And then, not only was it all over as soon as it had started, but Chris imagined, falsely it transpired, that he heard a car that sounded like his wife's car. So Natasha had pulled clothes on haphazardly as she dashed downstairs and fled. I assured Natasha that people had lost their virginity in much worse ways. Of course she agreed, but it had felt desperately disappointing at the time.

It was another thirteen years before she and Chris had sex. After that disastrous Saturday morning they still met and kissed and cuddled, but they never tried to go further than that. Two things happened which seemed to mark the end of their relationship. Both to do with letters –"if only there had been mobile phones," Natasha sighed. First of all Chris's wife found one of he letters Natasha had sent him , and later Natasha's father opened a letter that Chris had sent her during the summer holiday between the end of Sixth Form and her going to Uni.

Natasha's father was furious. Natasha was his only child. He doted on her and her having an affair with an older, married man played no part in any future that he had envisaged for her. He threatened to go and see the College Head and have Chris dismissed. Natasha pleaded with him not to, and he agreed this only on the condition that she never saw or spoke to Chris again. Chris never knew this, so when, after months of silence, in the Christmas holiday break when they bumped into each other, Natasha scurried by, head down, without saying a word, he was totally confused. Natasha admitted that the break from Chris had not been too difficult for her for she was at Uni, making new friends. (Once upon a time it had been mooted that Chris might quit his job and go with her to Uni, but they both had known that realistically it was never going to happen.)

As Chris and his wife no longer attended the Methodist Church she had assumed that Chris had got over her and had moved on. For thirteen years there had been no contact between them. And then, one cold November evening they had met. "It actually felt like Fate." Natasha was married to a German and lived in Berlin working as a translator. She and her two small children visited her parents twice a year. Five o'clock on a Saturday evening they had finished their shopping and were walking towards their car when, almost literally, Natasha bumped into Chris. He too was out shopping, looking for ghee, in a part of town he hardly ever visited. "I can't tell you how excited I was."

They made an arrangement to meet for coffee on the following Monday. That went well: there was hand holding and much laughter, and they had been in touch ever since. At first it was just cards at Christmas and Easter and a coffee when Natasha came to the UK. But then Chris divorced and had his own flat in which he lived alone. That was when Natasha visited him one evening. "I told my father where I was going and he affected not to mind – he was getting old, he could have forgotten about us." But even had he objected nothing would have stopped Natasha going. She was excited and knew what would happen. Apparently what took place in Chris's bed more than made up for their first disastrous sexual encounter. She blushed as she remembered the evening and a wistful faraway look overcame her.

After that, whenever Natasha visited the UK, one evening was set aside for their love-making. It seemed the right and most fulfilling thing to do. Fleeting visits meant sex on the living room carpet in the house which Chris had by now bought. More often there was time for leisurely love making. And once when Jurgen, Natasha's husband, had been away on business, Chris had stayed with her and the children in Berlin. "We just got on so well. It wasn't just sex. I really was happy that he was back in my life." Anniversary cards had developed into meetings and, two or three times a year being completely inadequate for their needs, they now phoned each other quite regularly. Even once when Natasha was on her way up hill to see the Oberammagau Passion Play. Natasha had remained a convinced Christian, but she saw nothing wrong with her affair with Chris. She knew that Chris had other girl friends. She also knew that her marriage to Jurgen was almost over. "Some things are so special. You know within you they are right."

Her marriage finished. She and Chris had never talked about ever getting permanently together, although, she had learned quite recently from the stories he had sent her, he had thought that her divorce would bring them closer and might well lead to marriage. But at the time Natasha knew nothing of these thoughts of Chris's. Apparently he also harboured the notion that once a marriage is over each partner should be permitted to feel and grieve their loss: it simply is not the right time to ask someone to marry you, for that could be construed as taking advantage of that person and exploiting their grief. That was Chris's thinking. He was giving Natasha time.

But of course Natasha was not privy to Chris's thinking. She felt alone in the world – whereupon, enter John. I should probably have mentioned earlier that Natasha knew John before she knew Chris. They had gone to the same Church and their families were friends. And Natasha and John had been on the way to becoming boy and girl friends before Chris had exploded into Natasha's life. Be that as it may, that Christmas after Natasha and Jurgen had separated she had come to visit her parents, and Chris was not around as he was visiting his parents "somewhere in the north." But John **was** around – taking leave from his job in Saudi Arabia. Both their families went to Church on Christmas Day, both John and Natasha were divorced or divorcing and were both feeling lonely and were free. They rekindled their relationship of thirty or more years previously. After the Christmas flirting they had continued to write and phone, and then on Valentine's Day John had phoned Natasha and asked her to marry him and move to live with him in Saudi Arabia. "I was so excited. I said yes without any hesitation. We kept quiet about it, but agreed to tell our families that Easter – it was an early Easter. That actually was fun, telling John's parents. I dressed up in a full burqa and John introduced me to his parents as his bride from Saudi. I was silent and submissive. They didn't look me in the face or they would have seen my laughing eyes. As it was they looked at each other and, despite their obvious dismay, they reached across with their hands to welcome me. And then I took off the burqa." Apparently there was delight all round. The marriage was fixed for the summer and Natasha was then going to move out to Saudi Arabia where John had still two years to go on his engineering contract.

Before that Easter the only other person that Natasha had told about her upcoming marriage was Chris. He was the friend and lover she could confide in and, in retrospect and with the clear evidence of the stories he had sent her, Natasha realised how distressed he must have felt. But he didn't show it. He offered his congratulations but did curtail the phone call. And, if his autobiographical stories can be believed, he put down the receiver and just howled and howled. So much for his respecting grief and loss and standing back and behaving honourably! Natasha went to see Chris that 'Easter of the Burqa' as she referred to it. John had flown back to Saudi the day before she returned to Berlin, so on her last night she paid a visit. It was slightly awkward between them, but they had a drink and toasted Natasha's forthcoming marriage and then made love for the last time on the living room floor.

And that was the last time they had met. John had no knowledge of Chris's existence so, she explained to Chris on the phone, she could not invite him to the wedding – "but I did send him some wedding cake which – if I can believe every detail of one of his stories – he threw into the garbage bin." After John and Natasha were married she never spoke on the phone again with Chris, but the Christmas and birthday cards continued to be exchanged.

And now he was dying and she was full of guilt and uncertainty and no friend with whom she could talk.

When I suggested that it was perhaps selfish and cruel for Chris to dump this stuff on her, Natasha rushed to his defence. She was so glad he had done. She and John had got on so well at first: there was the excitement of living in the very different culture of Saudi Arabia and they could share their love of motorbikes too. "It was a new world." But the novelty had worn off and, now they were back in England and had been for ten years, John had settled into the role of being old and she was fearful that she was doing the same. She often had thought of Chris, the feelings that she had had that they were meant, destined, to be together. She had speculated what her life might have been like had they lived together. She was very unsure whether it would ever have worked out, for he was much more of an intellectual than she was, but she was pretty sure that it would have been more exciting than her current life. "There would have been energy," she mused.

I asked her whether the stories she had received were works of romantic fiction, but no - the details of their relationship were all set out accurately and the feeling behind them was so strong. They had not been written recently. The only error which Chris had made in one story was to paint a picture of John, whom he did not know, as a villain. Natasha had cried when she read them – "there was so much love there." She was concerned that she had missed out on what was meant to be her life's love journey. At times she sounded like a giddy, romantic teenager, almost an alien person from the elderly, staid, overweight woman in front of me. I felt myself sympathising with John; it appeared that he and Natasha had, at the very least, been comfortable together until the literary, and contextually loaded, assault that Chris had made on Natasha.

What I said to Natasha was that I thought she could thank her lucky stars – which for her meant God – that she had had such a wonderful experience of love with Chris.

Not everyone has that and she should acknowledge the specialness of it and celebrate that. She got that but couldn't quite shake the thoughts of what might have been. I hope I wasn't too rough with her when I kept on reinforcing the importance, for all of us, of living in the present. "No regrets, coyote", I wanted to say to her. And I pointed out that her current lifestyle seemed pretty good to me.

As for Chris's funeral, whenever it would be, I dissuaded her from even thinking of attending. He now lived two hundred miles away. "Why risk the marriage you have for a marriage that you never had?" was my question. I was sure that Chris would be delighted with the note she had sent him before she came to see me. No more needed to be done. This affair of hers, which started fifty years ago, was simply a romantic adolescent dream. After she had unburdened herself I saw my role as snapping her into reality.

I don't know how far I succeeded, and I am not sure that was what she wanted from me. Some people just want to talk, and she was one of those people. We had just the four sessions together, and a fortnight after we had finished she dropped me a note –"Chris died last week. Funeral tomorrow. I'm working with John at the Food Bank tomorrow. Destroy this note!"

I duly destroyed the note! But I often think about Natasha. It is true that she had sunk into a non-demanding old age, probably prematurely. She could, though, look back on her life and know that she had experienced a real burning love. Not everyone can say that – and she was fundamentally far too kind a person to even hint of what had been – and what might have been – to John.

(I never did ask her how she came to be named Natasha. She was of a generation whose daughters were called Mary or Susan or Marion – Michelle or Nicola at a pinch. But Natasha?!)

HANNAH

Hannah was single and unexpectedly pregnant. That was the dilemma which, by talking with me, she hoped to be able to resolve. I believe – and I said so to Hannah – that women are best equipped to talk about child birth and abortion. But Hannah and I had a counselling history, going back to when we trained together. At that time we did some co-counselling together and over the years we have on occasions used each other when either of us needed to talk about difficulties or problems, usually emotional or relationship issues. So, despite my being male, she chose and trusted me with her unburdening.

Because of our past work together I knew of her childhood, of her aged parents, her wayward elder brother that her parents could not control, of her parents' lack of ambition for her which meant that Hannah had had to fund, by working in various shops, her time at University. She had studied Psychology, lived in an all male environment and had eventually lost her virginity in a tent in the Lake District to a fellow student with whom she then lived for a while. I knew that as well as working independently as a Counsellor she also worked as a Supervisor of a hostel for a Christian charity.

This – and quite a bit more – I knew. I should add that she is considerably younger than I am, some twenty or more years. And I should admit that she and I, in the past, had had a sexual relationship. That had happened initially during our counselling training and, as such liaisons are strictly forbidden, we had had to keep it hidden. The relationship continued for a further two years. The point I am making is that I knew Hannah pretty well. Not only did I know her but I liked her and wanted things to work out for her.

What I did not know about Hannah was the state of her current relationship(s). Before she went into that she explained that she had only recently discovered that she was pregnant and had been for twenty weeks, so, if an abortion was to be had, a decision had to be made almost immediately. She felt embarrassed that she had not until now realised she was pregnant and had been taking alternative treatments for an eating disorder that had caused her belly to swell. She was almost certain who the father was, but that in itself was a problem for she was not in a relationship with him, though she had been two years previously. I pointed out that it was unusual for a pregnancy to last two years. She did not appreciate my attempt at humour and explained what had happened.

Initially she held back the name of the man who had impregnated her. "It doesn't matter right now. It's simply a matter of me and the situation I am in. Do I want this child and all the complications and ramifications for the rest of my life? I need to talk. I need you to listen." And talk she did. Until eight months ago Hannah had, for a year, been living with a Canadian therapist. They had shared a flat that came with the hostel she was managing. His main motive for being in England was to obtain British citizenship. He and Hannah had met on a course and got on, so in the first place he was hoping she would go through the ceremony of marriage with him. Hannah had been happy to go along with that and they had also begun a sexual relationship. Then one day she had woken up and realised how much she was being used. From that moment she had denied him access to her body and had told him to return to Canada. "We never married. He never got his British citizenship." Three weeks later he was gone, quite an angry man, but "I put up with him having sex with me on his last night."

That had happened three weeks before, as she saw it, she had the fateful sexual encounter with her old lover. It had all been over between them for two years, during which time they had maybe talked three or four times on the phone. All friendly. And then one October afternoon, when she happened fortunately (or unfortunately) to be at home, there he was, knocking on her flat door. Her ex-lover had driven along for a meeting, had got stuck in traffic, the person he was meeting had thought he wasn't coming and had gone elsewhere, so here he was with an hour or more to kill. He had dropped by on the off chance of finding Hannah in. Hannah had been pleased to see him; they had talked and when conversation stalled they had got into bed together and fucked. "It so felt the right thing to do. It was good." And that was it. He had driven away and that had been her last sexual liaison.

"He doesn't know I'm pregnant." And then Hannah got fed up with saying "he" and told me the name of the putative father of her child. Sean. It was a Sean I knew. He was a fellow Counsellor, now Therapist, who had trained with Hannah and me. (It can be quite an incestuous little world this world of therapy and counselling.) I expressed some surprise, but on reflection it made sense. Even when Hannah and I were together she and Sean were good friends. Indeed once – and I don't think they were drunk – they had suggested a threesome with me. As an experiment. I had rejected the proposal.

I thought that Hannah should at least inform Sean of his paternity and said as much. Hannah was adamant that it was her body, her responsibility and her choice. In addition she knew that Sean was in a relationship and she did not want to scupper that. Eventually, by using the argument that as she was still thrashing around for a decision and needed as many informed perspectives as she could get, I persuaded her to talk to Sean. She was reluctant to do so but succumbed to my view as she realised that there was no one else with whom she could discuss her dilemma. We set a time for our next meeting for a week's hence and agreed that Hannah would then make her decision.

When Hannah returned the next week I admit I was hoping that she would look at ease, having made a decision. In fact there was a wild desperation in her eyes. She had talked to Sean who had been horrified. Why now?

He was far too old to become a father again, and hadn't they had unprotected sex for years without any thought, or any outcome, of pregnancy? And what about this man from Canada with whom she had been living – couldn't he be the father? Those were his initial reactions. Wisely, I think, she had let him talk and then suggested they talk in three days' time when he had had time to reflect. Sean had been much calmer by then, but insisted that any child would be Hannah's responsibility, but if she could really assure him that it was his child and she decided to keep it he would make a financial contribution. But that was all. He did agree, though, that basically it was Hannah's choice.

I asked straightaway if she could guarantee that Sean was the father. What about the Canadian and his last night? Didn't that fit into the time frame of the pregnancy? Hannah admitted that it did, but they had had only anal sex.

Hannah had no picture of a future career path: what was worrying her if she kept the child was whether she would, emotionally and financially, be able to cope on her own. Sean's commitment of financial support had removed some of her money worries, but she wasn't sure whether she could be a mother alone. We thrashed it all out: her down-to-earth practicality and good sense would seem to be an asset as a mother. And she might need her friends, me included, to provide emotional support.

I could sense that she was moving towards having the baby and I didn't think the fear of an impending labour was a factor. Hannah was a big, strong woman: she could handle the physicality of childbirth. I think what clinched the argument for Hannah having the baby was when I briefly reminisced about when we two had been together: how we had always had unprotected sex and there had been no hint of a resultant pregnancy. But now, a chance one-off fuck, had produced this situation. I said something like: "It's almost as though this child was meant to be." I could almost see her mind working and accepting what I had said, and then her face lit up. All solved. She was going to give birth.

And give birth she did, some twelve weeks later. A boy she called Simon. I kept in touch with her and indeed once met Simon. He was a lovely, bright-eyed intelligent boy, with a gift for music. He had a pitch-perfect singing voice, but, probably more significantly, by the age of four he was already writing tunes on the keyboard. Hannah seemed happy. She certainly knew that she had made the right decision.

When Simon was five Hannah returned to me again professionally. She was fighting off depression. When she and I had been together I had seen her through a long period of depression which had seen her hospitalised, so I was well aware of this proclivity of hers. Depression can descend from out of the blue anytime, but Hannah thought she knew the cause of her current descent. There was no man in her life. She and Simon were closely bonded, but that was not enough. She had dated men since Simon's birth but everyone had backed off on hearing of her motherhood. She had decided that she needed the physicality and the companionship of a man and that Simon needed a more permanent male presence around the house. What did I think? I played devil's advocate, pointing out strongly that the male of the species was not the essence of reliability and that 'he' could imperil whatever peace of mind that she could even now access. I resisted the temptation to say that a dog would be a more dependable companion but that certainly crossed my mind. I also resisted the temptation to propose that if she thought it would help for her just to have sex every fortnight or so then I was perfectly willing to help her out. I think she had made up her mind – that she was going ahead with a serious quest for a man – before she came to see me; she merely wanted to share her thoughts with someone who knew all about her depressive tendencies. At the end of our one-off session together she seemed to think that I had somehow given her the green light to proceed with her plan to explore serious dating agencies, ones that *you* paid your not inconsiderable amount of money and *they* made your choice. Her search would in itself, I knew, create enough energy to at least temporarily relieve the fear of succumbing to depression.

I had enjoined Hannah to come again to see me in a few weeks' time so she could talk about her experiences in her quest. I don't think that suggestion was for my own titillation; I knew Hannah could be naïve and suggestible, and I genuinely wanted to help prevent her from making a mistake. When she came to see me three weeks later she had no need of any approval, or indeed any felt response from me. She had found the very man! Only half a dozen years older than she was, very fit from constant cycling, considerate, a steady engineering job, a virgin, only child – what could be better?! And he was totally cool about Simon. Amazed at her enthusiasm, I ventured to ask if there were any flaws in this man. That is when Hannah conceded that he was "emotionally illiterate", but she had no doubts that he was open to her education in that area. Her depression, which she now called 'the blues' had vanished. For her life was beginning again. I didn't have the heart to raise my concern about someone being 'emotionally illiterate'. Hannah was happy and I was happy for her.

We exchanged social pleasantries over the next few years, and I met this man, Douglas, a couple of times. He seemed pleasant and insubstantial. More to the point they seemed happy together and had two children, both girls. I was very surprised when, one morning, eight years after our last, pre-Douglas, session together, completely out of the blue, Hannah called me. It sounded urgent and I had a free slot that afternoon when I could accommodate her.

She was not so much distressed as angry, an anger mainly directed towards herself. Like so many people, fearful of rocking a boat that was still afloat, she had, when she had last seen me, held back on expressing her dissatisfaction with her life. "Trying to make the best of a very bad job," was how she expressed it. Once she let down the dam that had been holding in her feelings they all came pouring out. The floodgates had opened. I listened, trying to make some sense of the torrent of words and feelings. After the initial outburst Hannah slowed down and I was able to piece together in my mind what had been going on over the years. Reassembled in chronological order, her life had developed along the following lines.

At first she had been delighted with her acquisition of Douglas. He was Mr Dependable: you knew exactly when he was coming home; he was tidy around the house; he put the bins out and he cut the lawn – and, under Hannah's tutelage, he had become a passable lover. At the beginning he was lacking in self-confidence, but then after his first daughter was born and Hannah cut down her working hours almost to nothing, meaning that his was the income was almost totally relied on, Douglas grew in confidence and began to assert himself.

Simon was the main sufferer. Perhaps it was that, after being for so long the main focus of his mother's life, he found himself competing with not only Douglas but his new sister, perhaps - but there was something which deep down caused Simon to rebel. Perhaps it was also adolescence. Perhaps. Whatever it was Douglas could not handle what he saw as Simon's sullen resentment, which he expressed by kicking in the panels of doors and pulling down curtains. An intelligent, articulate boy had turned into an inarticulate monster. Douglas could not handle it and threatened to beat Simon into behaving. "And Simon was always more intelligent, more quick witted than Douglas, much more. Simon would play around with words and ideas that were beyond Douglas. He could run rings around Douglas. He would be having fun, being a little cheeky. Douglas thought he was being deliberately rude and would demand an apology or order Simon to his room. I would always step in and take Simon's side." Apparently Hannah had almost come to see me then, but they found a family counsellor who was more expensive than helpful. It was Simon who one day "just returned to normal."

As a family group they had pretended 'the year of discontent' had not happened. But it had left a legacy. It had highlighted Douglas's emotional inadequacies. Another daughter had been born but that had not brought them all together. Simon had started at University but Douglas was now laying down rules for their elder daughter to adhere too, and threatening punishment if they were not obeyed. He was talking of himself as being the man of the house and the decision maker. After the birth of their second child Hannah had been short of energy and settled for a passive role. Douglas was still a reliable bread-winner; they had a nice little semi-detached house; it was a comfortable bourgeois life.

Then a fortnight ago Hannah had woken up and was struck by the intellectual and emotional paucity of her existence. "It was like a thunderbolt of realisation," she explained to me. She wanted more from life. She needed to go out and work. She needed more intellectual stimulation –"I wanted to go to the theatre and not just read copies of Douglas's Readers' Digest when he had finished with them." She wanted a relationship in which there was a mutual sharing of feelings – and expression of them. And she was angry with herself. She had settled for mediocrity. Douglas had from the beginning been an eeyore kind of person and a bore. Never had an interesting or original idea. Emotionally he had never grown up. How could she have stayed in that relationship for so long? What a fool she had been! At the beginning Hannah had felt in control and Douglas had been kind. Now the kindness had gone and Douglas was playing an outdated patriarchal role. She wanted out.

Often in my role as a counsellor it is my responsibility to challenge my client in order to ensure that she is certain about the correctness of her perspective. In this instance I felt I had no need to do so. Indeed my response immediately was one of affirmation, encouraging Hannah to get out of her stultifying relationship. I had known Hannah for decades, known her as bright and intelligent, sensitive and caring. Over the years she had so compromised that she was at risk of losing her core self. It was good to see her alive and passionate again. I did not fear the return of depression.

That's it really. I continued to be an outlet for Hannah to explore and understand the mistakes she had made in that central relationship. And we agreed not to dismiss its importance completely as it had produced two daughters who, difficult as each was, she would not wish to have denied life to. These daughters remained with Hannah so it was Douglas who moved out of the family home. A dozen years down the road, both daughters are at University and Simon is a successful musician. Hannah has a flat in a Care Home which she manages. Covid has been difficult for her but she lost none of her inmates. Organising and caring, with a cheerful hands-on approach, that, I think, is the right role for Hannah. I think she has lost her appetite for men and is succeeding in being self-sufficient.

EMILY

"You'll never guess who's coming to see me tomorrow," I said to my friend Hywel. We were having our weekly Wednesday drink together.

"I don't suppose I will."

"Well," – and I paused and looked him firmly in the eye. "It's Emily."

He spluttered over his pint, as I half knew he would.

"Emily! My ...."

"Yes, your Emily."

He was silent for a moment. "I'm amazed. She's the most self-contained person you're ever likely to meet. I can't imagine why..."

"Well, she is."

Let me explain. First of all "**your** Emily gives the wrong impression." Emily was her own person, didn't belong to anybody, and she was in a relationship with someone called Josh, not in a relationship with Hywel. Though she sort of had been once. And both in and out of his cups Hywel from time to time expressed his ongoing love, from a distance, for her. Which is why I bent my counsellor's oath. Of course I should not have disclosed details of my clientele to anyone, but Hywel was a fund of knowledge about Emily. Through Hywel, I told myself, I would be able to tune into Emily before she arrived in my consulting room and thus would be better prepared to counsel her. By talking to Hywel, on whose discretion and his love for Emily I could rely, I was simply doing my homework. That's how I justified my indiscretion – and also, I must admit, I wanted to see Hywel's reaction.

That reaction was mainly one of concern. He kept shaking his head in disbelief. "Emily, of all people," he muttered. In fact, apart from affirmation that Emily had always seemed too self-contained to seek help, I got very little new knowledge or insight about her that evening. So what I am going to say – which is the knowledge I had of Emily before she came to see me – is based on what Hywel had confided in me over the years.

For Hywel had been well smitten with Emily – as indeed he is to some extent to this day. They had initially bumped into each other at some social occasion and had recalled their previous meetings when as teenagers their paths had occasionally crossed when the local girls and boys schools had had combined functions. I remember Hywel telling me so excitedly about this later life meeting with Emily and how he was going out with her on a date. She was petite, black haired, beautiful in fact, with amazing eye contact. These were Hywel's words, and then he described how tight fitting and moulded to her backside were her jeans –"I just wanted to stroke her."

In fact Hywel never got to stroke that backside, though he and Emily went out for some two or three years. When I say went out I mean that they regularly went for an Indian meal together, went for a drink together, went to the cinema together. They even went on holiday together, a week in the South of France. Socially they were a couple, but that was as far as it went. Very early in their relationship Emily said to Hywel that if they ever had sex she thought she would eat him for breakfast, but that they must never have sex for that would mark the end of their relationship. Hywel treasured their relationship so much that he didn't want to risk imperilling it.

I know that on their French holiday they shared a (large) bed and remained chaste. I know that on that same holiday Emily was happy to stroll around the bedroom half-naked and to talk to Hywel while she was lying in the bath. Hywel was convinced that she wasn't deliberately trying to tease him or provoke him. He simply respected her wishes, though he felt emasculated. He discovered later that, all the time she had been seeing him, Emily had been having sex in the afternoon with someone that Hywel had never heard of. "But why should you have known of him?" countered Emily. "You and I are just friends."

Hywel shared a good deal about himself and Emily, but to focus too much on what he said would be to place the emphasis on Hywel and both the pain and joy she had given him. We must stay with Emily. She had got her degree in Humanities and had various jobs, including secretarial work, college lecturing and running an employment agency. She never stayed long in any job. When quite young she had married a long-distance lorry-driver; she had enjoyed both his presence and his absence. He was a big man, she a little woman, but, even though they had now been divorced for thirty years, they were still not only good friends but also Emily was a frequent visitor to his house about half a mile from hers. There had been no children. By choice, I believe.

Emily was gifted in many ways. She could act; she could sing; she could talk knowledgeably on a range of subjects, including politics. Where she was a Corbynista and a virulent critic of what she saw as the fascist state of Israel. The acting amused her for a few years, as did the community singing. But she never stayed long at anything: there were so many fascinating things in the world. She was not, though, a dilettante: whatever she was into she explored it and gave it her full attention. Hywel still met up with her for lunch very occasionally and said that her most recent area of interest was psychology and especially psychologists like Jung and Assagioli. Nothing like your standard government sponsored (and therefore discredited and cheap) CBT.

This was the picture I got from Hywel. "You're in for a treat," were his parting words. "You lucky devil!"

"I look forward to meeting her," was my reply. And I truly did. I realised that I had seen her through Hywels' rose-tinted vision. It was the real person I was meeting the next day.

She cycled to see me, which gave her cheeks a rosy hue. Her hair was greying and quite thin, her chin was pointed, not unlike a caricatured witch's chin, She was no longer the young beauty that I am sure Hywel still saw her as. But hell she was in her late sixties and her brown eyes still sparkled and her tight-fitting jeans served to emphasise a well-shaped and preserved figure and what some would call her fitness. It was a still attractive woman who was seated opposite me. I felt blessed, smiled and thus encouraged her to start talking.

Emily knew that I was a friend of Hywel's and her first concern was to get an assurance from me that all she said would be treated with complete confidence. I gave her that assurance – and she started.

She just wanted to talk. That's what she said. Her life style imposed certain constraints on discussing all the things that were going round and round in her head. By talking freely she hoped to gain more control over her thoughts and hence be able to bring some order and acceptance into a life – "and find more time for myself." Emily explained to me why she felt she had no other option but to talk to me – "a last resort. For once I can't quite do this on my own." Her basic problem was that her partner of some fifteen years (who had replaced Hywel and had added the missing sexual element) was profoundly deaf. They communicated well enough, but it was a slow process and therefore at times frustrating. Additionally they did not live together so when they did come together so much had happened and built up in Emily's head that she wanted to discharge her thoughts like a geyser but was reduced to a trickle by Sean's deafness. She explained that living apart was a completely amicable arrangement and that she and Sean could – perhaps as a result of this arrangement of separateness – still be said to be in love.

Emily had a sister and brother-in-law who lived close by, as did her elderly mother. She couldn't burden her mother with her problems (and indeed her mother was a part of one of her problems) and somehow she never was able to get on the right wavelength on the isolated occasions when she was alone with her sister. She felt constricted when talking on the telephone and, yes, she would have shared it all with her ex-husband only he had gone off to a Greek island for a month. So she came to me. It was a long explanation and she seemed to be needing to justify this visit, as though she was showing a weakness. She was giving herself a hard time and angry that she had to come to me, for she would under normal circumstances expect to be able to sort out her own stuff without any intermediary help. I really was a last resort and that indicated personal failure: that was the very strong message I got.

Emily needed to unload. She had an ancient aunt and uncle who were in separate nursing homes and she had an elderly mother and all of them needed her constant support. "There's not a day goes by when I don't get a phone call from one of them, needing something." She didn't begrudge the time and help that they demanded of her "if only that were all!" In addition, though, there was an ongoing dispute with her neighbour who proposed to build an extension which would turn a part of her garden into shade. And then there was the Labour Party. She had been a lifelong member but had recently been expelled for posting comments that were critical of Israel on her Facebook page. "Where do I find time to get on with my collage?" She explained that she was creating her own deck of tarot cards, intuitively putting pictures together to express the essence of the tarot card. She had started the Ace of Pentacles three weeks ago and she had not found the time or energy to do any more work on it. "I'm screaming inside my head, for air for me. I have to talk to someone about it."

I suggested she go through these subjects one by one and tell me not just what was happening, but her emotional responses to the situations. She needed little encouragement. In the first place there were these three relatives she was caring for. There was her aunt, her mother's sister, and uncle, both in their late eighties. They had lived in Scotland most of their married life, but had returned to live near Emily's mother and family just five years ago. And almost immediately they had both become ill, necessitating, eighteen months ago, they're both being transferred to nursing homes – and there had been no nursing home that could accommodate them as a couple. They had no children and it became the responsibility of their unmarried niece to respond to their needs – as I have mentioned, not a day went by without a phone call and a request – and also to bring them together by taking them out for coffee twice a week. "I wouldn't begrudge them the time – and they are grateful – if this was the only bit of caring that I had to do."

There was, though, in addition, her mother. It couldn't yet be labelled dementia, but her mother's memory was going and she was experiencing frequent bouts of depression. Emily's sister did help out a little with her mother's needs, but it was left to the elder daughter to give massive support and time to her mother. In addition Emily's brother had recently had a breakdown and, although he had now returned to his solitary home, he had stayed with Emily for four months. "Four months of privacy, of my own quiet time lost!" But even though he had now left, Emily did not feel that the burden of responsible caring had decreased. "I know I have to do it. I realise they need me, and I don't really begrudge the time I have to spend with each and every one. But overall it's getting me down. Where is the time for **me**? And look at my Birth Chart: where does it say 'carer' in it?" A rhetorical question: no need to answer.

There was the neighbour too. He was proposing to build a conservatory which would extend the length of his house and so blot out the sun from Emily's patio. Having initially tried to reason with him, she had written to the Council, voicing her objections, and then had consulted her local Labour councillor, someone she knew well. And the latter manoeuvre had not been helpful in so far as she had been informed that she could only object within the parameters of the building law and regulations and this conservatory didn't meet any of the criteria for its building being denied. The whole disagreement had escalated too:

she had uncharacteristically lost her cool on one occasion and had sworn at the neighbour, and he had retaliated by playing blasts of loud rock music at odd hours of the day and night; not only were the wall of her semi-detached breached but so was Emily's creativity and her sleep. Again she had involved the Council and its noise abatement officer, but his interference had simply increased her neighbour's antagonism without reducing his musical barrage. I listened sympathetically and thought to myself that maybe I could help in this dispute, and, even as I thought this, Emily was bewailing the possibility that she might have to move house.

Almost without a pause for breath Emily moved on to her next bugbear – the Labour Party. In the first place she was appalled at how what she saw as the principled, vibrant Labour party, attractive to young idealists, the party that had gathered around the basic socialism of Jeremy Corbyn, was being dismantled by the stodgy right-winger Starmer. That was breaking her heart and her spirit. Moreover there was a personal element to her disillusion: she had shared a similar fate to Jeremy Corbyn in relation to their criticism of the Israeli government and her support for a viable state of Palestine. Similar but different in that she had been expelled from the Party. She explained that she frequently posted on her Facebook page articles critical of the fascist, apartheid, racist state that Israel had become and so had incurred the wrath of the Jewish media police. "This conflation of criticism of the Israeli government with being ant-Jewish has been so successful. The Labour Party has feebly fallen for it. It's outrageous. I am free to criticise any government in the world, but not the Israeli one. It makes no sense. It very nearly pushes me into the arms of the anti-semites. But not quite," and Emily ventured a wicked smile. I had no problem in genuinely agreeing with her about how the Israeli government has effectively censored debate and discussion. But surely not the Labour Party. Could she not appeal against her expulsion? Well yes, she could. But it would take time and energy, both of which she had not got. And besides she wasn't at all sure she wanted to be a member of the Party as led by Starmer. When her period of stress and exhaustion was over – if ever it would be over – she was planning to join the Greens. "They are motivated by idealism."

I assured her that realistically she knew that the current period of stress and exhaustion would sooner or later come to an end. She smiled wrily. "I know. But it just doesn't feel that it will. Sooner I hope – I feel suicidal at times. Those were words of despair but I was pretty sure that they were merely words. This strong woman was never going to kill herself. I asked her when – with a strong emphasis on the 'when' – this immediate crisis was over what she wanted to do in the freed-up time. "So much," she answered. "For one thing I've got this project of making my own personal Tarot deck. I'm collaging and photocopying and making my own cards. It's great fun and I'm learning so much about myself. But it's a fortnight since I last was able to get on with it. I haven't even finished the major arcana yet: I've still got The Tower, the World and The Hanged Man to do. For all practical purposes I have to use my Greek myths deck. That's what I consulted before I came to see you. You came out well, very feminine." Emily grinned.

I grinned back. "Anything else besides the Tarot pack that is in abeyance?"

"Oh everything. I'm not writing up my dream diary. I really believe in Mindfulness and living in the present. I just can't do that. It's one anxiety after another. I suppose I feel cheated. Anyway. Thank you for listening. I needed to get all that off my chest. I won't be coming again and, if I do, I'll almost certainly want some real therapy. But you have been helpful." And she nodded her thanks again.

Her last words as she swept out of my room were: "And, of course, not a word to Hywel."

I watched her retreating form. Only a gentle sway, but it was enough for me to see why Hywel had fallen for her in the first place. Oh, that backside!

GABRIELLE

The majority of the interesting and, by and large, lovely people about whom I am writing I encountered in a counselling setting. *This is simply not so with regard to my German friend Gabrielle. I am building my portrait of her from a number of very personal encounters that we had. I had little opportunity to delve into her early personal and family history.

Some would say that it was by chance that we met. Gabrielle would emphatically deny that. What happened was that she came across to England as a member of a group specially selected by the German government to advance their English. It was a high-flying group who were here for a two week intensive course. The language school that ran the course shared a building with the Adult Education centre. It was a Monday evening, and the German group, having completed their first day of studies, were having a welcoming drink together. Having just completed my Art History evening class studies, I was having a quiet solitary drink at the bar, something I had never done before, when I was confronted by Gabrielle.

"Hello! I knew I'd find you."

I looked down on the short woman with laughing green eyes. She looked up at me and smiled in a completely open way.

"I beg your pardon?" (I can be so English.)

"I've been looking for you. It's a long story, but if you take me home, I'll explain."

"Home?"

"Your home."

"But…"

"Come on. Finish your drink and we'll go."

For a moment I was bemused. I looked more carefully at this young woman. She may have been thirty, some fifteen years my junior, but that was not what registered. I noticed her round face and her round breasts; she had drawn attention to her legs by wearing highly coloured horizontally striped rainbow tights; but what continued to strike me were her eyes – they were laughing and welcoming, laughing at my confusion and welcoming me to her world.

I was in between relationships at the time, living alone in my flat, which was only a stone's throw from the building in which we were talking. Uncertain but content to be led by this deep-voiced, non-threatening stranger, I knocked back my drink while my new friend picked up her anorak from the back of a chair. One of the teacher's was talking to her, looking quite angry. I just heard her say, "No John. I made a mistake. This is the man I'm going home with." John gave me a filthy look and muttered something like "poacher" as I joined Gabrielle and we left the building together. I felt a lot of eyes on us.

Outside she introduced herself as Gabrielle and I introduced myself as Rhys. She didn't say a word on the way to my flat, but grabbed hold of my arm and snuggled up. I said nothing either, but when I looked down she was always looking up at me and smiling contentedly. Those eyes, those eyes!

I shut my door behind her, leaned back against it while she pressed herself against me.

"We have to do this. I'll explain later."

"You mean you want to fuck?"

"No, not that word. We make love."

I lifted her off her feet and into my arms and carried her to my bedroom. We undressed each other quite slowly and then made love, initially fervently and then slowly. It was good. I felt at home and, she assured me later, so had she.

We stayed in bed talking and Gabrielle explained her behaviour, assuring me that what she had done was atypical, and that that was the first time she had picked up a stranger in a bar.

"But you weren't a stranger." She was an astrologer and – something to do with Jupiter and her Ascendant if I remember – she knew she had to come to England and find me. Somehow she had heard about this fortnight course for high-flying students and had blagged (my word) her way onto it. She was a nurse in a cancer ward with little money. She knew that the alignment of the planets was such that now was the propitious time for her to meet someone from a past life. And as soon as she had seen me….

Astrology and past lives…… All new to me. If anyone else had said this to me my innate scepticism would have kicked in, but somehow, lying naked with Gabrielle, I accepted what she said without demur. She must have read something in my face, though, for then she laughed and assured me that that was not the story she had told the German English-learning scholarship interviewing board. I never did find out what convincing story she must have told.

Gabrielle didn't stay the night with me – in fact during that fortnight she always returned to the family with whom she was lodging. We must have made love four or five more times during her stay, but what was eventually more important was her impact on my thinking.

It is not too strong an expression to say that I was bewitched by her. I listened to her and she opened my hitherto conservative, would-be rational mind. First of all it was the astrology which explained the timing of her visit. She felt her life had been stagnating and she needed a new, refreshing impulse to invigorate her and reset her life's compass. The heavens had shouted loudly that the present time was ripe for such a focus. Hence she had bestirred herself to get chosen to come on this English language course. That she had chosen to come to England was, she admitted, an intuitive impulse, nothing to do with the stars. But, she then explained to me how important were the alignment of the planets at one's moment of birth as they indicated the direction of one's current life – not just the direction but they gave you the tools to pursue it. The Birth Chart was a road map for one's life, and she felt herself at a critical juncture, not knowing which facet from all the possibilities offered by the Chart she should be following.

I heard all this and my initial scepticism must have shown itself through my silence. Gabrielle in response mentioned some of the great minds who had accepted the truths of astrology. I remember she cited Jung and W.B. Yeats and Louis MacNeice – two of them poets, not renowned for their rationality, but then I remembered Plato's saying that "poets are the unacknowledged legislators of the world." And then I remembered that it was Shelley and not Plato who said that. So I thought, in the words of Mandy Rice Davis, "he would say that, wouldn't he!" (Plato – of course! – was very critical on poetry on the grounds of its being unethical, unphilosophical and non-pragmatic. He saw poetry as pervasively harmful, spreading false views of nature and the divine.) But to return to Gabrielle and astrology. What convinced me of its validity was when she drew up my Birth Chart and talked me through it. Almost all she said I could relate to with regard to my aptitudes and skills. Without studying it at any great depth I have subsequently been convinced of the truths underlying astrology and, indeed, a major premise of this little book is an astrological one. Perhaps I should dedicate the book to Gabrielle.....

The validity of astrology was one idea that Gabrielle planted firmly in my mind. Another was the idea of reincarnation. Her belief- shared by the Islamic Sufis, the Christian Gnostics, the Jewish Hasidics- was that we all reincarnated many times in a quest to develop the divine within each of us so that we could eventually become part of the Divine, the ultimate benevolent source behind and thoroughly within the World. It's a difficult concept, I find, and maybe it was Wordsworth who put it best when he wrote:

"Trailing clouds of glory do we come,
From God, who is our home."

That's from his *Intimations of Mortality* and is a wonderful poem. Be all that as it may, what mattered with regard to Gabrielle and me was that reincarantionists believe that when we die we go to somewhere called the bardo where, with the help of wise guides we decide when and where, for the purposes of our spiritual growth, we are next going to take carnate form and hence when we should be reborn with a Birth Chart which optimises our purpose and growth. From time to time the individual loses track of his/her sense of lifetime purpose, and that is when (s)he is reminded of it by being confronted by someone from a previous incarnation whom we immediately recognise. For Gabrielle I was that person. As soon as she saw me she recognised me and my immediate unquestioning acceptance of her indicated my recognition too.

Ultimately Gabrielle and I did some past life regression work together, but what I want to celebrate this moment is the vitality and the fun and the complex life that was Gabrielle. I was what you might call single and available at the time, and I was happy for my life to intertwine with Gabrielle's. But to say the least it was never easy. She always had a married boy friend in her life. There was a time when the then current boy friend's wife died, and, for a couple of years, she moved in with him nominally to take on the role of caring for the children. I know she found this difficult and the children resented her – I suspect that the alacrity with which she moved into their recently deceased mother's bed was a strong contributory factor to that resentment. During those years she stopped her work of nursing elderly, dying cancer patients, but once the quasi-married relationship was over she returned to work. I visited her once in Munich, and she took me along to the ward in which she worked. So many machines to monitor, machines showing the data of the patients' body workings, and so many lonely, dying people to comfort. I am sure she did the latter part of her job brilliantly. Gabrielle took death - and life – seriously: she cared.

Yes I stayed with her once. I remember being in a pub where an enormous biker, someone - and Gabrielle never elaborated – from her past scooped her up, almost in the palm of his hand, and sat her on his knee. I remember drinking beer with her in a beer hall. I remember that she had a neighbour who took his chameleon on a leash for a walk every day. I remember too some of her art work: she was a painter who, on large canvases, painted esoteric dreamlike landscapes. She was a photographer too, a pretty good one. I recollect too meeting her mother: another small woman, but as neither of us had the other's language we made little contact. I learned that Gabrielle had had a brother who died aged sixteen. This was never even alluded to afterwards. Most of all, though, I remember feeling frustrated. The week I was with her in Germany we didn't share a bed and we had different body clocks: she would sleep till well after midday and I was (am) a morning person. I think her current boyfriend knew about my presence and she had promised him not to sleep with me.

That experience repeated itself years later when she stayed with me, for once all by herself. We shared a bed, but she told me from the beginning that she had made a promise to Jurgen (maybe; I do not recall his name- and it is not important) that we would not have sex. Of course I respected her wishes, but but but.... It was difficult. And then, when we arrived early at Heathrow for her flight home, sitting in an underground car park, she, as it were, rewarded my restraint by, out of the blue, reaching across and giving me the most amazing blow job.

I mentioned her staying with me by herself, for, as the years went by, she visited frequently in her summer holidays but usually brought a friend or two along with her. There was a year, though - in fact the one that followed our initial meeting- when she stayed in England for a year: she was once more following the dictates of the stars. She studied at a College of Art, only some forty miles from where I lived. I had great expectations of our relationship growing. But in fact, although we spoke on the phone quite often, she visited me only the once and I visited her just the once too. She was staying in a house by the river, an old almost mansion of a dwelling. And the man of the house – as I saw him a small, miserably dribbling obsequious man – was obviously besotted with Gabrielle; and his wife unsurprisingly was not very fond of her! She did manage to have a goodly number of us older men eating out of her hand. With younger men I think she had less of an impact. Indeed she phoned me on the night of yet another German victory over England at football. She had been at a small party, but when England lost the mood had turned nasty and, fearing rape, she had made a swift exit.

Gabrielle never lived up to my hopes and expectations. I knew she was a free spirit whom I could never have to myself. I learned that early. But I was disappointed that I did not see more of her alone. There was a time when, at home in Germany, she went for a number of weekends on a course, in a controlled environment taking LSD. She was full of enthusiasm for what she felt she had discovered, of the underlying divine nature of the universe. I think it was she who suggested that we had a weekend together taking LSD. Certainly I was all in favour, and to that end bought LSD from a local dealer. The weekend kept being postponed and postponed, with the LSD lying in a drawer. One day I realised that the promised weekend was never going to happen, so I took the drug alone. And it did nothing for me except to make my whole body stiff and my mind perplexed and gloomy.

Disappointing yes, ultimately Gabrielle was disappointing. But we had some marvellous moments together. Glastonbury was our favourite place: for me it was the Abbey, with its majesty and history, by which I was spellbound; for Gabrielle it was the Chalice Well Garden, with its beauty and serenity. But we climbed the Tor together and explored Wearyall Hill. Great times.

If I can digress for a moment I should add that one of my past life experiences took place in a particular spot in the Abbey – I stand there today and the tears fall. Quite simply I, as a young novitiate monk, aged fourteen or fifteen, was murdered by a monk who was jealous of my receiving another's attentions. I had a similar past life experience in Draguignan in the South of France. Again I was fourteen or fifteen. It was the sixteenth century and there was a feverish atmosphere of religious persecution. My mother and father and myself had been driven out of town and were hiding in a cave. My mother was ill and needed medicine and I was sent into town to get some. While I was standing outside the apothecary's window I was stabbed fatally in the back.

Back to Gabrielle! I remember driving into Glastonbury, holding hands, like an old King and Queen, returning to their kingdom. And Gabrielle placing on the mantelpiece in our bedroom a nine inch, thick red candle; it was never used but magically dominated the room. A room from which we looked up to the Tor. That in itself was magic.

Of course we were not a King and Queen, not even in past lives. We were both fascinated by the Arthurian legends, so we visited Tintagel (and the Witches' Museum at Boscastle where Gabrielle seemed at home – one of her most prized possessions was a large crystal ball. usually covered with a purple velvet cloth.) We walked round Cadbury Hill in East Coker, the site of Camelot, and I felt I could feel the presence of King Arthur and could easily imagine I was him. In fact Gabrielle often referred to me as 'her King.' But she was never a Queen. I see her as a Celtic elf-spirit, disguised in mud, grubbing through the undergrowth in the Middle Ages, hunting, foraging, scheming.

The one past lifer experience that we shared was of our being thirteen year old girls in Finland, and the joy we had running along a sandy beach together – and then Gabrielle was taken away and we never saw each other again. In this lifetime one of the most joyous things we did together was walking along the sands. I hear her laugh, deep-throated, encouraging me to join in; I hear her call me by my name, making it sound as though she were mocking me and accusing me of doing something naughty. It didn't matter what the weather was like as we walked the beach. Sometimes we walked together, more often apart. Sometimes we spoke, more often not – but the silences between us were resplendent with the power of loving and longing. Not loving and longing between us, but the shared loving and loving for a better, deeper, more spiritual world in which we could live together.

Gabrielle was (is) a gamine, although the roundness of her breasts somewhat belied that. Mainly she was small, her feet certainly were, but her footprints on the sand left deeper imprints than mine did. Her imprint on me? She was a wonderfully curious, New Age free spirit: she was open and unshockable, And the times when she snuggled closely in my arms were times of deep joy. But the fullness of the promises she held out to me seem more likely to be fulfilled in our next incarnation.

* I never acted in a counselling capacity with Gabrielle. The reason for her inclusion in this book is that I loved her and she introduced me to astrology.

ANNE

Anne was in her late sixties when she came to see me. She was seeking meaning and purpose in her life - that was what she told me. It emerged later in our conversations that before she came to me she had already spent time with a priest friend of hers, seeking answers. When she told me this it simply confirmed my thought that she had come to the wrong person. I never said this to her for I envisaged her realising this for herself very early on in our sessions and that would bring about a natural conclusion. She never made this realisation, but what I realised was that it was not meaning and purpose that she was needing, but, like the whole human race, love.

The outline of her story is as follows. She was born in Ireland of parents of whom she would not have a bad word spoken. She was the middle child, having an elder brother and a sister some six years younger than she was. When she was nine her parents emigrated to England to give their children better educational opportunities. Her eleven year old brother straightaway got a place at the local Grammar School, and two years later Anne was given a place at the local girls Convent School. We are talking early nineteen fifties when "blacks, Irish and dogs" were frequently told they were not welcome. Because of her background – and her accent – Anne did not fit in easily to a fairly posh girls' school. But she did say how wonderful were the nuns who taught her. Yes, she came from a strong Catholic background and indeed the priest she had consulted before she came to me was a priest/friend from her youth. At this later stage in her life, though, she was not a practising Catholic.

Anne achieved very respectable A levels and moved on to do teacher training. When she came to me her hair was mid-length and grey, but she assured me that in her prime it had been a striking, luxuriant red, sweeping down to the small of her back She had always been ambivalent about her hair for as a small child in Ireland she had heard her mother being commiserated for her daughter having red hair, but in later life it certainly made her attractive. You could not help but notice her. She overcame her longstanding feeling of inferiority and the resultant shyness when she acted at College, playing such parts as Pegeen Mike in *The Playboy of the Western World* and Alison in *Look Back in Anger*. She thought that acting and being seen helped her subsequently in articulating the leftwing radical views that, apart from to her family, she had up till then kept to herself.

These leftwing views took her to places like Grosvenor Square and the USA embassy to protest about the Vietnamese War and started a life of anti-government protest marches. They also took her to her first job, working for a humanitarian aid agency in Africa. Her very white skin meant that Africa was a difficult proposition, but she stayed there two years before returning to the UK to become an organiser and spokesperson for the agency. In her forties she changed agencies but remained in the same field of work, bringing aid to those in need in Africa. For fifteen years Anne chaired the organisation; she became a well-known public figure, often seen and heard on television and radio. She had a very distinctive clear and confident speaking voice, enlivened by the occasional Irish pronunciation – 'piano' for example. When she retired the Blair government wanted to make her a Dame, but she refused on principle: her socialism had no place for a patronising elitist system which still used what was for her the totally discredited appellation of British Empire.

You may remember that Anne came to see me looking for meaning and purpose. What she had told me thus far, about a life of service, seemed to me to indicate that certainly at one time of her life – in fact a considerable chunk of it – she had found a purpose and probably a meaning too. When she then went on to tell me that after retirement she had worked as a magistrate for ten years until she had perforce to retire at seventy and that after that she had been elected as a Labour Councillor (which she still was, working, she assured me, upwards of fifty hours a week) I could restrain myself no longer. I simply had to say that what was in my book an amazing life of public service would indicate that she had found purpose and meaning, though maybe not fulfilment. Anne was quiet for a few moments and then shook her head and said that never had what she was doing been quite enough for her. In her teens she had briefly flirted with the idea of becoming a nun and devoting herself to a different kind of service "but I knew that would not be enough." And all through her public service career she had known that what she was doing was not enough. She admitted that her strenuous work ethic had probably been to hide the void she experienced: life had no meaning. Twice she had been in a clinical retreat to help her overcome depression. Anxiety was a condition with which she had lived all her life; she conceded that there was never a time when her mind had not been able to find something to worry about obsessively. From time to time this got on top of her and she succumbed to depression.

It felt like an ontological or spiritual issue to me. I could see clearly why she had seen her priest friend. I really wasn't sure that I could help, but I realised that she had told me nothing about her personal life, her personal relationships. Zilch. I asked her about them.

Her response was a halting one and, unlike when talking about her professional life on which subject she spoke freely, it was only in response to a good deal of prompting from me that the following details emerged. From an early age she was used to being surrounded by boys as her sociable outgoing brother had always invited plenty of friends round to their house. So the male of the species possessed no alluring mystery to her, and her own pallor and bright red hair made her feel unattractive. On the other hand her young sister, all black haired, rosy cheeked and sparkling eyes, **was** seen as attractive and had what Anne quaintly chose to call "gentlemen callers." Anne was seen as the intellectual, her sister Jenny as the beauty.

It was only when she got away from the family home and went to college that Anne realised she could be seen to be attractive, mainly because of the luxuriance of her hair. This certainly made her noticed, and boyfriends duly followed. I have no idea when or how she lost her virginity: she was very tight-lipped about matters of sex – such things were not on her agenda, at least not for discussing with me. There was certainly one young man around during her college years. She was learning and growing in confidence. Then when she returned from Africa and her career took off she did get into a stable relationship. His name was Michael; he was tall, slim and bearded and apparently they made a striking couple. He worked for the government in a capacity that was never vouchsafed and I never explored.

Anne and Michael had what many would describe as an unconventional relationship. Each was bent on following their career, each had their own house and they lived a hundred miles apart. They came together most weekends and for holidays. It seemed to suit both of them. After this arrangement had been in place for fifteen years, they decided that it was time to marry, to formalise what their relationship had become. And that decision had been disastrous. Within three years they were divorced. They had tried to be more conventional and spend more time together. That had meant they got on each other's nerves and they had begun to role play and lost both spontaneity and freedom.

Anne explained to me that she had kept in touch with Michael until he died of cancer ten or so years ago. Thinking it was his funeral to which she had been invited, she attended his memorial service and found that, presumably to meet the wishes of his recent partner, she had been completely airbrushed out of Michael's life. "I can't tell you how much that hurt." And the funeral had already passed without an invitation. Anne thought that for twenty years she had been important in Michael's life -, indeed she was pretty certain that she had been - but she had had no acknowledgment, no appreciation. Her feeling of unimportance had been refuelled.

She had married again some ten years ago. I questioned her about this: had her not previous experience of being married deterred her from taking the same step? Anne explained how different it was. Her second husband, Dan, didn't begin to have the looks of Michael; there was no coup de foudre. He was an older, retired university lecturer, fairly stable and laidback – and that offset an anxiety that increasingly took over Anne's waking hours, which, she explained, as she had great trouble in getting in any sleep at all, meant most of the time. They had similar interests and were comfortable enough together, and basically he was a kind man. But basically she had settled for a marriage of convenience – "as you do when you are older."

I casually mentioned that she had no children. She stared at me and this set off a surprising and, I must confess, not altogether convincing reaction. After she had returned from Africa and become established in the UK, she told me, it was then she felt had been the optimum time for having children: she would have been about twenty nine. But that was the exact time when her mother's dementia had so deteriorated that she could not live on her own. Her father had died eight years previously; both her siblings were married with small children; Anne, as a single woman, was given the responsibility and task of taking her mother into her home and caring for her. So for three years she had exhausted herself in doing, as she saw it, two jobs. She explained that she never really slept during that time for her mother was a bad sleeper – an hereditary trait that Anne herself had inherited – and would, if possible, let herself out of the house and wander off. There was also a major issue of having to wash soiled clothes and bed linen every day.

When Anne could no longer look after her, her mother had gone into a home and died not longer after. "I always see those as my missed child-bearing years," she informed me. Not long after that she had met Michael and he had never wanted any children. "I had no option but to become a career woman."

Talking of her mother led Anne into bewailing how little gratitude her siblings had shown her for the onerous task – "on their behalf" – she had undertaken. "I don't think they ever appreciated what I had done." This in itself led Anne to complain about the lack of love and appreciation her brother and sister had shown her. Were she in trouble they would, of course, come dutifully to her rescue, but there was no spontaneous warmth. And whereas it was possible that her maternal instincts could possibly have been fulfilled through her nephews and nieces, she was never given the time and opportunities to get close to them. This lack of children in her life resonated deeper as she got older and saw how valuable were the relationships her husband had with his three children. Many of her friends were so insensitive too, as they would prattle on about their grandchildren, not realising how they were tapping into her well of frustration and, maybe, her perceived failure as a woman.

Not that women needed children to fulfil themselves, she insisted. Just as for men the world should offer a myriad of opportunities for each distinctive individual. Gender should be irrelevant. But it wasn't, and she would fight for women's rights of equality wherever they were denied: whether it was freedom to walk the streets at night or equal representation in the board room. She saw herself as a feminist – and yes, of course, she was. For herself, though, she would have liked to have had children and was angry that friends would trample on what was for her a sensitive area of regret. The assumption was that she was a contented career woman who had consciously foregone a family for a career.

When I pressed her Anne conceded that neither her mother's needs nor Michael's reluctance were to blame for her childlessness. She was prepared to take the responsibility, but it rankled nonetheless. I suspect it rankled more the older Anne had got as she saw children as a source of love. And perhaps they would have given her the appreciation that she craved (though, of course, that is never guaranteed).

Appreciation, love, meaning – these were what Anne was seeking. I should have thought that her socially and internationally involved public life would have given her the appreciation she craved, and indeed the proffered Damehood seemed to indicate this, but she batted away those thoughts of mine. She had done what she thought was right for her to do, using the skills at her disposal. And yes, she supposed she had had some acknowledgment and appreciation, but it was for the roles she played not for the person she was. It was in her personal relationships that she did not receive the love and appreciation that she felt she deserved. Domestically, in the home, she thought she did eighty percent of the work and took a hundred percent of the responsibility and it wasn't even acknowledged. But, she admitted that she would not have it any other way, for she always had to oversee and be in charge.

We shilly-shallied around using the word 'love'. It was always in the forefront of my mind, but Anne remained reluctant to discuss intimate details of her life. All she would say was that she thought that she had never experienced 'real love' – apart from her parents, and they had shown it by sacrificing their comfortable life in Ireland to give their children much better opportunities in life. It was by deeds, not by words or physical contact, that her parents had shown their love for their children. "It was a generational thing," Which is true but times have moved on, and I was very conscious when, at the end of one of our sessions, I attempted to give Anne a hug; she went rigid, kept her hands by her sides and gave me nothing back in return.

That's as full a picture as I can give of the Anne who came to see me. Neither her professional life nor her personal life had given her the sense of purpose, meaning and fulfilment for which she was craving. I could not fix that for her. I did venture down some philosophical, spiritual paths with her, though, hoping, without any real confidence, that such exploration might help.

It happens from time to time that a client asks me what I think or believe. As I am sharing what I hope is a relationship of mutual trust with my client I feel duty bound to respond to such queries. Anne asked me if I believed in God. I asked her to define what she meant by God. But no, she had asked me first – how would **I** define God? Pressurised by what I felt was an intimidating fixed stare I stumbled out my thoughts about it being a kind of miracle that the universe existed; it is equally miraculous that there is life on earth and that here we are as intelligent beings. We could guarantee that the sun would rise in the East each day and therefore there was some kind of benevolent spirit or energy which supported life. That was as close as I got to the concept of God.

Anne wanted to know how this affected my every day living and were there moments when I personally felt connected with this God. (She kept using that word: it is a word that I eschew.) I began to mutter something about sometimes being transported by music and seeing the sunrise in a mountainous landscape, but she cut me short. "No, I mean God speaking directly, unambiguously to you." I acknowledged that in adolescence I had thought that had happened – but that was a time of a disturbed mind.

That was when I lost her. She did not walk away immediately, but I saw her eyes glaze over. She changed the subject for the closing ten minutes of our session, and then left. She phoned later to say that she would not be returning. I could understand her decision. If even her priest friend had failed I was never likely to succeed. Anne wanted unambiguous certainty. What she needed to meet her craving for recognition and appreciation was for her to be so special that she was one of those chosen ones, one of those to whom God spoke directly. She had not rid herself of her Catholic indoctrination and she was doomed consequently to eternal suffering. I think what she really wanted was to confess to some minor indiscretion – like snogging a Protestant or a Tory – and for a priest to flaggelate her while she ecstatically cried out "Mea Culpa."

VENETIA

I first met Venetia when we were both out running. Early each morning I used to set off and, for variety, I used to juggle around my routes, never taking the same route more than twice a week. One of my routes took me round the nearby large lake and, it seemed, that each time I did so I came across this young woman earnestly running. After three or four encounters we raised our hands as we passed each other and maybe would have smiled had we not been focused on the exercise we were doing. I am very nearly a fair weather runner, so I was a little dubious about setting out that particular morning as it was mizzling under a louring sky. I'm glad I decided to go.

My route that morning took in the lake. The rain was now much more substantial and I was beginning to regret my foolhardy decision to go out at all when I came across a bench on which Venetia was sitting and, as I got closer, I could see that she was crying. Tentatively I sat down next to her and asked if I could help. She just shook her head and continued to sob. We were both soaked through and she looked completely bedraggled. I imagine I looked similar. We sat quietly for a minute; she was still sobbing, taking huge breaths of air.

"Look," I said. "I can't leave you here like this. Can I walk you home? Or run with you, if you like?"

She shook her head. "I don't want to go home."

"Well, what can I do?"

"Nothing, just leave me. I'll be all right." She gestured me to go away.

Reluctantly I stood up. I sensed I was felt to be one more threat. "Look," I said as I edged away, "I'm a counsellor. If ever I can be of any help .." I gave her my name and invited her to look me up in the phone directory.

She nodded. "Just go away."

That was it. I went on my way, and as I left the lakeside I looked behind me. The bench was empty and there was a disconsolate figure trudging off in the opposite direction.

In the next three weeks of early morning running I think I did the lake route five times, and each time I looked for the sobbing young woman. No sign of her, and I was wondering what had happened to her and thinking how unlikely it was that I would ever see her again, when an appointment was made by someone called Venetia. The name meant nothing to me, other than that there was a well-known, and attractive, race horse trainer of the same name. Venetia …. It sounded posh.

It took a few seconds before I recognised her, as she smiled confidently at me before she sat down. This was not the slim, bedraggled, white legged waif I had encountered by the lake; this was a well-dressed, well spoken, confident young woman. Very attractive too. My first thought, as soon as I recognised her, was what had happened to her, what transformation had taken place, since I had last seen her? But I let her do the talking.

She began by introducing herself as Venetia and apologised for my having seen her in such a state by the lake. She wouldn't normally have gone running on that particular morning – the weather would have deterred her – but she just had had to get out of the house. And then she had been hit by the enormity of her situation and had broken down. That was when I had seen her. "I was at my worst, my lowest. Thank you for trying to be kind. I'm afraid I didn't appreciate it at the time." But she had remembered my name and she was here to say 'thank you' but also she wanted to avail herself of my counselling skills. I was delighted: she was considerably younger, and more attractive, than my usual clientele.

She came straight to the point. Her problem was men. Her relationships with them. She explained that when I had seen her by the lake that day she was distraught because of a violent row she had just had with her boyfriend. It had not just been words, but physical violence too. On that bench she had resolved to leave him, realising that that would take courage and she might well take a beating, but she had to get out. The beating and threats had followed, but she had escaped and was temporarily living with "mummy and daddy." She blushed when she said those words, and that made her even more attractive. Venetia had a very cherubic face, with green sparkling eyes; she was wearing a scarlet beret at a jaunty angle and light brown knee-high leather boots. I was maintaining appropriate eye contact, but I was well aware of her jeans and jumper and the fact that the top two buttons of her white blouse were undone. It took all my experience to focus on what she was saying. Obviously she was attractive to men and I could see that she might have hassle problems. But surely she should have gone to a female counsellor? Why me? I should be so lucky??????????????

Anyway, I concentrated as well as I could. The man she had recently left, she explained, was her "bit of rough." She was initially intrigued by his cocky self-confidence. He had been cleaning the windows of her flat and had grinned at her every time he had seen her as she went from room to room. It was a contract window cleaning for which she paid a direct debit monthly, so there was no need whatsoever for him to ring her door bell when he had finished. Other window cleaners had simply walked away. This man, though, did ring the bell and, when she answered, just stared at her, undressing her as he did. Venetia was fully aware that she was playing with fire, but when he came to the point and asked her out, it was only for a split second that she hesitated. "It was like an adventure into the unknown, sailing the seven seas of lust," is how she described her feelings.

His name was Rick and he took her to an Indian restaurant. He talked a lot about football – Chelsea was his team – so when he groped her under the table she found it a welcome distraction. After that they had gone to a pub round the corner where there were a number of his so-called mates. Five men and her drinking together, and she had enjoyed being the centre of attention and clearly Rick enjoyed being the envy of his friends. When one of these friends, though, started coming on to Venetia, Rick lost his temper and started pushing the friend around. And they left. "Of course I invited him in, nominally for a coffee, but we were, as they say, very soon 'at it.' He didn't hold back and I was well and truly fucked. Maybe the best ever." Rick moved in with her soon after that, and he became more demanding and almost brutal in his love making. "He was using me." And also very controlling. "I went out to work. At the Estate Agents. Otherwise I never went out on my own – and I didn't see my family or friends." That morning when I saw her wretched by the lake, she had asked him to leave and he had just laughed at her and then hit her and said he would offer her to his mates and would invite them round that evening. Fortunately he had had a window cleaning round that morning, so she had thrown together as many possessions as she could and left. "He's still living in my flat. But that's another matter."

I made some remark to the effect that it was a good job her parents lived nearby and she could return there. But Venetia shook her head. Hesitantly she suggested that maybe her problem with men stemmed from her relationship with her father. It was a wealthy family – he was "something in the city" – and she was an only child. Her father had been "over fond." He would touch her and stroke her, never anything beyond that, but she was aware of her sexuality from an early age and did not know what to do with it. An all girls boarding school and the shared lusting fantasies about every young man the girls saw did not help. But then came university. And Venetia had experienced the sexual pull she possessed over the male of the species and had luxuriated in a very active sex life. "I was just enjoying myself. It was all new to me. I didn't have a regular boyfriend. I played the field. Not only was I incapable of making choices, I didn't want to."

She had left university four years ago with a degree in Marketing, and through her father's influence she was now working for a very large estate agency, with a view to moving into management. She had become less interested in sexual conquests, but now had found an alternative form of thrill seeking – by backing race horses. "I used to ride. Horses are such magnificent creatures. I want to own a race horse one day." Venetia acknowledged that gambling was a substitute for sex. "It's throwing yourself into the rivers of chance, and hoping you can swim to the shore." She didn't think her gambling was out of control, but feared it might become that way, just as her sex life had once become. "I don't have an anchor," she confessed. "I'm drifting. I need some stability. That's why I'm here. I need your help."

I began by remarking on the water imagery she had been using. Was she aware of this? "Oh yes, 'alone on a wide, wide sea' and 'oed und leer das Meer'. Desolate and empty, that's me. And I'm bobbing helplessly around, terrified of going under. I really do fear 'death by drowning.'"

"And, here you are," I replied. "And not waving, but drowning."

"Exactly."

We agreed that she was good at waving and drawing attention to herself. She had looks and she dressed well. On one level she was an only child clamouring for the attention of her peers. At boarding school Venetia had done some outrageous things in order to get attention; she gave me the example of flying a suspender belt from the school's flagpole, a stunt for which she had nearly been expelled. But her charm had triumphed in the end – as, she commented, it almost always did. And she wasn't going to dress down and become dowdy for anybody. She was happy to be noticed, but unhappy that this made her vulnerable to male predators. "I want to give, I want to please." I asked her to hold on to that thought – we would certainly return there, but I needed to pick up on her literary references. Coleridge and Eliot, and obviously being familiar with my Stevie Smith reference. In my experience estate agents and poetry were an ill-assorted match.

"I love literature. Got an A at 'A' level. Wanted to study it at Uni. But daddy said 'No.'" Apparently his absolute concern was that his daughter should be able to make money so she could support herself. He did not see that English Literature would lead to a well-paid job. Studying marketing had not stopped Venetia reading. So here I was with a young woman with imagination and the human understanding that literature gives you. Her personal qualities were wasted in working as an estate agent. I said so.

And Venetia agreed! I had hedged my non-acceptance of estate agents by talking about "in my experience" and "superficial charm" and "sell their grannies to the highest bidder", and that my experience was perhaps nothing to go on, and that perhaps estate agents were fundamentally good, honest, salt of the earth people. Maybe my own bad experience had led me to make a totally unwarranted judgment of them. …Venetia just laughed and said that I was not wrong.

We talked together about the malign influence her father had had and was having on her, not merely sexual but with regard to her future too. She had to escape from under his influence, and yet here she was, driven back under his roof, needing his protection. That, though, was not going to last. Once she had got Rick out of her flat … And in truth that was going ahead. One day soon she would be free.

It was at that moment Venetia looked me in the eye and said "Will I ever be free?" At first she meant she was frightened of Rick and also the influence of her father. We spoke of the need to escape geographically, somewhere hundreds of miles away, and then we spoke of changing her career. For me when Venetia said "I want to love and be loved; I have so much love to give", that was the key to her. Up till now she had, as young people are wont to do, seen love mainly in sexual terms. I put it to her that there were so many different kinds of love and I mentioned philia, storge, philautia and agape. Of course I was leading her, but it was Venetia who put together philautia and agape and realised not only was she lacking in both but that, almost certainly, they were the way forward. If she really cared for and loved herself she needn't make herself available to almost anyone who expressed an interest in her – she was worth much more than that and, as she said, laughing, "I know those murky waters so well. The fun has gone. And the deeper you get in the greater the danger." Her laugh was a bitter one.

Once she had become at ease with herself and was respecting herself Venetia could focus on where what she began to describe as a "universal love" could be directed. A charity organisation – say for the homeless or perhaps working abroad. Wherever that would be it needed to be a long way from home.

It took us a couple of session to come to this conclusion. When I say 'us' and 'conclusion' it was, of course Venetia who came to this conclusion/understanding, and it was something that Venetia had known deep down all along; it simply needed to surface and be acknowledged and verified.

While Venetia both began to respect and love herself and to begin looking for alternative and altruistic employment, there was this still question of her growing gambling addiction to deal with. Wary of what she had learned about herself from her need to go the extra fathom with regard to her sexual panorama of experiences, what concerned her most about her gambling was that she might one day similarly go to extremes. At the moment she was happy at the stakes she used and the amount she was losing. "We all lose." She didn't want to stop gambling. "It's a wonderful thrill when your horse wins," but she was concerned at the growing amount of her time that was occupied by studying form and then investing and this might well lead to that feared overindulgence. She knew about the concept of addiction as an illness. But neither did she wish to become a nun nor never gamble again. Moderation was seen by us both as the middle way. That we agreed upon and, at the end of our last session together, it was agreed that Venetia would check in with me every two months and tell me all that was going on in her life and how she was in control. I was of course available at any time too if needed.

In our last session together I had shared with Venetia that I too liked to play the horses. That was a mistake. There are reasons why counsellors are advised to be quiet for most of the time, and it's not solely to do with enhanced listening. The client's focus is diverted from herself if she takes an interest in you. A few years previously I had been trapped into going to a charity concert for a local hospice with a client. I had expressed an interest and she then turned up with a ticket, sitting next to her. I felt I couldn't reject her. It was an embarrassing evening as I coldly rebuffed advances that were made.

That was all in the past. I determined that from then onwards I would never accept a social invitation from a client. So when Venetia's eyes lit up and said that we should attend a race meeting together I should have declined immediately. But I hesitated: she was an attractive young woman, and it could be fun.... That hesitation was taken as assent, and before I knew it a date had been set in three days' time to go to an evening meeting at Chelmsford. I had all kind of mixed feelings about it, but whatever happened I thought that Chelmsford was sufficiently far from where we both lived for us not to be seen together. (I was unsure whether our being seen together would have enhanced or tarnished my reputation!)

I picked her up in my car. I think she had already had a drink; she was certainly excited. It was a winter's evening so she was warmly wrapped up but she looked gorgeous. I tried to be in counsellor mode and suggested that we set a limit to what we would invest in each race – not more than

£10 a race. That was agreed on. There were not too many spectators which meant that getting access to a bar and a drink was easy. Venetia insisted that all drinks would be on her; the whole evening was her way of saying an extra thank you to me for having been so helpful. I had a couple of drinks with her and then, as I was driving, settled for soft drinks, but after each race Venetia downed alcohol. By the end of the evening she was well and truly drunk.

I remember little about the horses. I don't think we either lost or won much. The only horse I can remember was called Papa Stour, whose name Venetia made some me-related joke about. I don't recall whether or not it won, just that we backed it. No, my strongest memories of the evening were of a young, attractive, drunk woman who was increasingly all over me: she cuddled whenever she could, grabbed fleeting kisses and looked at me with pure lust. She leaned on my shoulder all the way home and her hand was on my thigh. Of course she wanted me to invite her in and of course she wanted to fuck. Nothing could have been more obvious. And, of course, there was a part of me that wanted to avail myself of what she was offering, but she was drunk and I would have been taking advantage of that. If she had stayed sober would I have turned her down? Would my counsellor role have kicked in? We shall never know. Outside her parents' house I had to get out, open her car door and almost drag her out, while she whimpered "Please take me home with you."

I slept uneasily. I knew I had done the right thing but I also fantasised about what I had denied myself. I wondered if I would hear from Venetia again. I did, three days later. Just a note: "Thank you for everything. And for refusing me. I was testing you. If you had taken advantage of me, I would have known that all your words were just words and that I could ignore everything we had agreed. As it is I do think my days of excess are over – be it sex, gambling, or, indeed, alcohol. Never again. Thank you."

JANET

There is an advantage to having my consulting room some twenty miles from the sleepy town in which I live; it provides anonymity for my clients, most of whom in fact travel those twenty miles to see me. It also means that I have moved amongst most of them for years and know, or at least have an instinct, about them. I agree that it is possible that this prior insight might lead to a hasty pre-judgment of my clients. Obviously it is something I try to avoid, and I like to pretend that each person I see has a tabula rasa when they start out on their journey with me. But in all honesty this is rarely the case.

Some of what I knew about Janet I had acquired from playing her at squash. We belonged to the same club and twice, in competitions, we had to play against each other. I beat her each time – quite easily in fact – but that is beside the point. She was a determined player who never gave up; she had racket skills and an astute brain but lacked a certain speed and finesse. In her time she had been a decent tennis and hockey player – which befits the games' teacher she once had been. Some women, playing squash against male opponents, wear short skirts and deploy sexy smiles – any ruse to get points, but Janet was not of that ilk. Her white clothes were functional. No one could ever describe her as sexy.

Yet it was sex that had thrown her and her husband together, she explained to me. They had been teaching at the same school at the time of the Clivedon/Christine Keeler/Stephen Ward/John Profumo sex scandal had broken out. It had been comprehensively covered in the News of the World, and the following day the school staff room did almost nothing but talk about it. All of a sudden a barrier had been broken: you could talk about sex, and, then, inevitably, practise it without there having to be any secrecy around it. Larkin (Philip, not Pop) was spot on when he averred that "sexual intercourse began in 1963."

By the time Janet came to see me she was in her seventies and her marriage had long been over, but in the course of our sessions she told me about that 1963 sexual awakening. She had gone to the rugby club bar with her fellow sports' teacher, Paul, on the Tuesday after the News of the World's pretty comprehensive reporting. Christine Keeler was still being talked about; there was a feeling of licentiousness amongst the mainly male rugby players and she batted away a number of suggestive suggestions and clung to Paul. But Janet had been aroused, and as Paul walked her home she pulled him to her, body to body, and kissed him passionately. And Paul pushed her away – she later had realised that Paul was gay.

What Paul did, though, the next day was to tell James about Janet's behaviour the previous evening and opine that "Janet was up for it." So was James. He invited her out that very evening, responded to her invitation for a late night coffee in her room and they lost scarcely any time in fucking. A certain liberation had taken place and sex was at last out in the open - but it was still linked to marriage. It was not until 1967 that the necessity of marriage following sex lost its moral imperative. So in 1964 Janet and James married. Quite a stylish affair, she told me, but I have no details.

It was many years later that James told her about Paul having offered her to him, as it were, "on a plate." By this time their marriage was as good as over in so far as sex had long since departed from their shared activities. It had gradually faded away after the first few months and, in their search to conceive, it had quite early on become a chore. Janet was initially disappointed at James's apparent lack of libido and went through a phase of wondering if he was gay, but as time went on and she found evidence of a number of affairs he had had or was having, that theory proved false. Maybe he no longer found her attractive or maybe it was the natural progression/regression of marriage when it comes to sex. Janet chose to believe the latter.

They did have a child, a daughter, but could conceive only the once. Adoption was mulled over as a possibility but ultimately rejected. For fifteen years they bumbled along as an apparently happy family unit, and then James dropped the bombshell that he wanted a divorce.

For Janet this announcement was out of the blue. She claimed not to have seen it coming, though I believe she had deliberately refused to countenance any breakup as a possibility. She could be very blinkered, needing to focus on her own concept of reality and trusting that things would continue in an orderly traditional fashion.

It was not the breakup of her marriage, though, about which she came to see me. That had happened fifteen or more years previously, and she had got over it. Janet had developed her dress making skills and was heavily into gardening, two things which, she claimed, had languished when she was married. She had had a couple of brief relationships with men soon after the collapse of her marriage, but now she relied on what she said were her countless good women friends. Probably stemming from her marriage when, she claimed, that she had done nothing wrong and its failure was all the fault of her husband who had always had a roaming eye, she now saw everything from an extreme feminist perspective. She saw all men as weak and perfidious. I often wondered why she came to choose me as a counsellor, but I put that down to the traditionalist that was a strong part of her. I think eventually when she dispensed with my services she did turn to a female counsellor, but that was months later. Her counselling pattern merely echoed her relationship pattern.

She came to see me as a result of the breakdown of her relationship with her daughter Michelle. The breakdown had actually happened some four years previously. Michelle had broken off contact with Janet as a result of Michelle's seeing a psychotherapist "who must have had her own agenda." Michelle had not stopped her grandchildren from seeing their grandmother, but required the presence of her father James on such visits. Janet had always thought that Michelle would "come to her senses", but despite her offers to see her daughter and "all would be forgiven" and they then would be able to carry on as though this hiatus had never taken place, her offers had been rebuffed. She had, a year ago, stopped trying to contact her daughter but the pain would not go away. Hence her visits to me.

Janet liked talking about herself: I know so much more about her than I will reveal in this essay. I cannot think of a single instance when the story did not lead to the ultimate glory, or at least justification, of her behaviour. Even with regard to childbirth; she was told how brave she had been and the midwife had said that she had never seen anyone as brave. She had taken the midwife's encouraging words to heart and believed the compliment.

That, of course, links with her distress at being ejected by her only child. Living in the same community I had known Michelle as a child. She had been very determined and stubborn like her mother, but had also inherited much of her father's more freedom-loving outlook. As a teenage she had rebelled mainly through punk music and fashion – she had needed to shock. As an adult, though, I had had no contact with her. I was told that she was an aspiring novelist and painter – and happily married. That was all I knew.

From Janet's perspective all had been going well with the extended family set-up until her grandchildren came to stay one weekend. It was after that that Michelle had severed their relationship. "She took exception to my punishing my grandchild, Simon. He was being silly and wouldn't behave himself so I put him on the naughty step. I was just trying to instil some discipline into him. He needed it." Michelle had been unhappy about this demonstration of grandparenting skills (and values), and, I surmised, this had reminded her forcibly of her treatment as a child at the hands of her mother. I asked Janet about how she and James had parented Michelle.

According to Janet Michelle had a world of freedom. "James didn't believe in discipline. He wanted her to have the freedom to learn from her mistakes. All very well in theory, but she was a girl and I knew the things that could go wrong. So I spent a lot of time talking to her and explaining what was appropriate behaviour. James did none of that. Even when she was a young child it was me who had to do the disciplining." Which, she said, included the naughty step.

Janet was adamant that she had always been there for her child. Some years ago Michelle had had a major cancer scare and Janet had been prepared to drop all she was doing and care for her daughter and take over the running of the household. It had fortunately been a rare case of an initial misdiagnosis so Janet's services were not required. "She seems to have forgotten what I was prepared to do for her," commented Janet on Michelle's subsequent behaviour. She thought it was just too cruel to be cut off from Michelle's family's life especially as she had been so involved in it. "They needed me –and now they pretend they don't."

I couldn't change Michelle's behaviour, but I thought I might be able to change Janet's. I began by saying that I was surprised she had not persevered with her relationship with her daughter. To which the snapped-back response was that she had given it two years and that her niece, with whom she now had a close relationship, agreed that it was up to Michelle to make the next move. I then suggested that in any falling out there were always two sides to it, and I wondered if she could contemplate that she might be partly responsible. I got such a withering and scornful look. "I have always been there for her." She just couldn't contemplate that she might have done anything wrong.

Then two things happened – one by chance and one I contrived – which helped me understand more about what had been going on between Michelle and Janet. The chance one came about through a walking group to which Janet and a good friend of mine belonged. I was having a social drink with my friend when, apropos of nothing, she suddenly said: "I walked along with Janet the other day. She suddenly got out her phone and showed me pictures of her grandchildren and was almost tearful. I was amazed. I had always seen her as someone who didn't have a single maternal bone in her body."

I nodded and moved the conversation on, but note had been taken. The other relevant encounter was one I engineered. I did know Janet's ex-husband James a little and so I contrived to meet him and ask him casually how Michelle was getting on. His face lit up: "Oh, she's better than she's been for years. She reckons she's regained her independence. You know she's separated herself from her mother. I feel sorry for Janet, but, you know, she does tend to take over things, and Michelle had to take the drastic step she's taken. She had to assert herself. Maybe they'll sort out some accommodation in time. Maybe. In the meantime Janet is telling everyone that Michelle has taken leave of her senses. I try to disabuse people of that. Anyway, she really is fine. Thanks for asking."

I really don't think James fed me this information, knowing that I could be counselling Janet. I don't think Janet was seen as someone who would ever accept advice, let alone go for counselling. As I write this down I realise that Janet in fact almost certainly required advice rather than counselling. She must have seen me as a potential magic wand. Counselling demands the individual look inside themselves and you the counsellor help facilitate the process of self-understanding. Whereas Janet was prepared to **talk** about herself, her capacity to question herself was very limited. But it was not as simple as Janet being on an ego trip. I have had a client who came to me each week and rabbited away about everything without looking closely at anything. I realised she had some sort of crush on me and that was her sole motivation for coming for counselling. I terminated our contract. It was different with

Janet: no way did she have a crush on me and she constantly claimed to have lots of friends and was never lonely. I tried to question this last statement but she brushed my attempts aside. She appeared so self-confident on the surface. I knew beneath the veneer there was a very frightened person, but she was never going to acknowledge it. You could say that I failed in my attempts to bring out the frightened child and that I failed, despite our dozen sessions, to help Janet become self-aware.

But I learned a good deal about her. I was not unsympathetic towards her, but I could not break down the pretence that she could do nothing wrong. To admit that would initially to have been to destroy the image she had of herself and the image she wanted to show other people. If only she could have faced her demons and doubts and have been prepared to fall apart ... before a healthy reconstruction based on reality and fallibility ...

So where did this self-perpetuating image come from? From what Janet told me over our time together I have pieced together the following story. Her background was solidly middle-class and aspirational: her mother possessed grace and charm and culture in contrast to her father who a self-satisfied, cultureless bully. He was a garage proprietor and that provided a reasonable enough income. Janet had an elder brother Christopher who was two years older. The two of them got on well enough but Christopher got to the local boy's grammar school at 11, whereas Janet transferred to the girls' grammar school after two years at the local secondary modern. She had always had to work hard for any academic results, but success at sport came more easily to her. Hockey and tennis were her fortes and, whereas Christopher went to university, it seemed to have been inevitable that Janet should go to a PE teacher trainer college. It was an all women's college and Janet thrived. "I always got stuck in," she told me.

That led to her first job, where she met and hastily married James – for sexual and conventional reasons. She was inexperienced visavis men; she had previously been out with someone else called James, but they had done little more than danced together and he proved to be gay anyway. She and husband James had a shared love of sport of all kinds and shared a conventional attitude towards marriage, which involved having children as soon as possible.

Janet's marriage really was conventional - that's the word that kept cropping up. Janet didn't have much of a sense of humour, but she smiled when she mentioned that her father announced her engagement in the Telegraph. James didn't object, although he was very much on the left of the political spectrum. His views had influenced Janet so she had soon seen herself as a Labour Party supporter, though not a member. She still saw herself as left of centre, though I did hear her once complain about the "shirkers and scroungers" claiming benefit.

I should have mentioned that when Janet was ten a baby sister was born. She was sent to a small fee-paying boarding school. "She was my father's favourite." There was no outward animosity towards kid sister Naomi.

I use the word outward advisedly. Janet was determined to behave well throughout her life, to do the right thing. Convention and decorum mattered within the family. And as a sportswoman you had to cover up any weaknesses you might have, for, if perceived, advantage of them would be taken. She had spent so much of her life pretending that all was well, that she eventually came to believe it: for her the carapace became the reality.

Which is why she was so shocked when James had wanted to leave her, and more shocked when her daughter also wanted to separate. They were not behaving conventionally. Beside the former had made vows to love her 'as long as ye both do live' and she had read and believed that the mother-daughter bond was the strongest bond of all. Both her husband and daughter had betrayed her and not just betrayed her, but had broken all the rules of conventional society. She saw herself as a victim. Ex-husband and daughter were the persecutors. I was cast in the role of rescuer – which I failed to fulfil.

I still see Janet occasionally around town. She exudes an almost belligerent red-faced confidence. It is possible, I suppose, that the hurt has gone - I am sure she pretends it has – but I doubt it. She has overcome her desertion by her husband by rationalising that all men are bastards, but somewhere within the daughter wound will be festering. She still plays tennis and cycles despite her being nearly eighty, and she is happy to take all plaudits for being wonderful for her age.

Janet possesses a lot of determination. She believes she has a host of friends, and she certainly does have one good friend with whom she holidays throughout the world. It is a Japanese woman, Noriko, slightly younger than she is. Janet met her when she came to learn more English at a local language school and Janet provided her with accommodation. Janet has subsequently learned Japanese and she and Noriko have travelled extensively together, not only in Japan, but have used their common interest in the Japanese language to explore other places where Japanese is spoken: Taiwan, Korea (South, of course), Hawaii and Brazil. She has become quite a globe trotter and is happy to accept the reputation of being "a game old girl."

That, then, is Janet. Strong minded, determined, friendly. But wedded to conventionality, of which the consequence for her is that she is wedded to pain. Self-righteous and completely lacking in self-awareness. If she could get over her self-obsession I am sure there is a generous-hearted woman that could be freed. I failed to free it. I do know, though, that she means well.

.

SALLY

"Chris, I need to talk to you. Can I come round – now?"

That's how it all began, how I was entrusted with most of the details of Sally's life. I say most because we all keep some stuff to ourselves, whether through embarrassment or vanity or just plain forgetfulness. And, quite often, it is because there is a deeply hidden pain, of which the perception is that it needed to be buried full fathom five and never again to be brought to the surface.

I had known Sally and her husband Jack and their three children for maybe twenty years. I think we first met in a train going up to London for a CND march. CND activities continued to draw us together, and then we progressed to playing tennis together. When I separated from my wife I believe the three of them continued to play the occasional game of tennis – but I didn't want to know that.

It was a miserable Saturday evening when she knocked on my door. I was watching some inane quiz show. Of course I invited her in and opened a bottle of Shiraz. She didn't immediately launch into the imperative reason for her needing to talk to me, but I had some idea as to where we were going – Jack was the problem or, perhaps, more accurately, Jack *had* problems, major problems.

That Saturday was the first of a number – five or six – meetings we had. Sally desperately needed to talk and share her current dilemma. I was trusted as a friend and she felt able to spell out everything that was going on in her life. I was not employed as a counsellor and, although she was clearly using my counselling skills, that felt fine: I liked Sally and wanted to help her.

I already knew that Sally had been adopted as a baby and that her adopted parents were elderly and God-fearing. There had been little joy in the household in which she was growing up and almost no physical signs of affection. Sally did not readily respond to the required meek submission, but it was not until she was a teenager and she discovered the local Youth Club that she began to blossom. There were boys there who liked her and made her feel good about herself and whom she was very ready to kiss and receive some much needed show of affection. Yes, she was good-looking but she also had a brain, and she realised that it was her brain that would get her away from the stultifying small village atmosphere in which she had grown up. So it was off to university to study History.

"I had a great time there. It was the sixties. I had so many inhibitions to throw off, and I sure did!" she told me. "I had already discovered boys, but I discovered alcohol as well. Drugs not so much. I joined the Labour Party and was politically active. Pro Castro. Anti-Vietnam War. All that."

Politically I could identify. I was a few years older than Sally so any sexual or other extravagances of the sixties had not impinged on my university life. We both got decent degrees, though, and both went into teaching. One of the things I had from our early CND days noticed about Sally was that when you greeted each other with a kiss, she always kissed you on the lips. Not just me! I took it as a sign of her emotionally sterile early life and her being starved of close physical contact, though it is a trait I have observed in many people who have been adopted.

Anyway, Sally was not as permissive as I might have given the impression. She had a strong mind and a clear picture of where she was going – which was mainly away from her childhood. And Jack helped. He too was a member of the Labour Party, active in CND and committed to education. Perhaps most importantly he also came from a similar small village in Shropshire. They had a mutual understanding of each other's needs and how each would not just understand but strengthen the other. They married straight after their degree ceremony and fairly quickly had three children, two boys and then a girl.

Jack had appeared to be the epitome of stability, the totally reliable husband and father. I think Sally occasionally played away – by which I mean that, from what I gleaned from the way male friends' eyes lit up when Sally's name was mentioned, that she was up for a kiss and a cuddle and a fumble – just possibly more – given half a chance. But Jack and her children were her basic stability. A safe base. There was never any doubt of that.

So it came as a devastating blow when Jack began to play away. And that is why in desperation that Saturday evening she called on my friendship.

Jack and Sally were both in their forties and Jack was the Headteacher of a small village school, with just four other members of staff. Both their sons had left home but a teenage daughter was still there. And as far as Sally was concerned the family unit was basically intact. Jack, an introvert who watched you with the eyes of an eagle, was going through a very quiet phase – but then that happened from time to time. And they were still having sex –"fairly bread and butter stuff, but what can you expect after all these years?"

The apparent harmony was disturbed by a visit from the police, wishing to talk to Jack on his own. Sally paced the garden, wondering what on earth was going on. The police were a good twenty minutes with Jack, and it seemed like an eternity to Sally. What on earth had Jack done? She couldn't envisage anything, so maybe he must have witnessed something untoward – but then why hadn't he told her? Her mind was racing all over the place. Hearing the front door slam, she raced into the house, where Jack was pouring himself a whisky. He looked shattered and answered Sally's clamourings with a wave of the hand, motioning her to sit down.

"You know Rosalind," he began.

"She's your young teacher."

"That's right. Well, it appears that she has been murdered. Strangled. The police just wanted some background."

"That's awful!"

And then it all came out that Sally couldn't know how awful it was. Jack just broke down sobbing. He began by saying how special a person Rosalind was, and under Sally's apparent unrelenting stare, he admitted that he had been having an affair with her. This scene had been played out a fortnight before she came to see me. In the meantime a man had been arrested for the crime of murder: the man was Rosalind's ex-boy friend who couldn't accept that Rosalind was 'seeing' someone else. No one knew who the someone else was; they had interviewed Jack in the hope that he might be able to shed some light. He had denied all knowledge but had confessed to Sally. Which meant she was carrying this burden of knowledge about her husband, which she had to keep to herself for fear of a barrage of adverse publicity and his almost certainly losing his job, and at the same time she felt her marriage had been destroyed. She was in a hell of a state and she had turned to me to unload and entrusted me with a secret that I had to keep.

The adopted child had been abandoned – again. She had thought that she had a secure base from which she could reach out, continue to explore further dimensions of herself and then always return to a home where she was loved. And she had been betrayed. Maybe Sally could have forgiven Jack the occasional fling, a meaningless one night stand. Maybe – she thought she could have. But she had experienced the depths of Jack's hurt and his confession that he had loved Rosalind. She wanted him out of her life, out of her sight, but there was a problem: if they split up at this moment in time questions would be asked, people might very well put two and two together and Jack would be revealed as having been Rosalind's lover. The sky would fall in on their children and on Jack's job. She had to stay with him, in the short term at least.

She wanted him nowhere near her and had moved into a spare bedroom. But "we still fucked." She thought it could be his way of trying to express some remaining love for her, but it always felt angry and brutal as though Sally was being punished. Sally endured it, hoping Jack would feel her distaste and his guilt at using her would increase. These days he fucked Sally only when she was on her knees; it was an animal coupling.

All this I was told. Sally was frank with me. With no one else could she share. I knew too that, once the furore over, the murder was over and the local press had done its worst, Jack would move out. In the meantime Sally's one and only emotional release was me. So I should probably have guessed what happened next – another Saturday evening.

I was alone. The bell rang. Sally was at the door. And she was dressed differently. No one could ever accuse Sally of being a sexy dresser, but this evening she had clearly tried. My eyes were immediately drawn to her legs where not only was she wearing black fishnet stockings but also a very short - and slightly crumpled – tartan skirt. Her hair was no longer controlled by the habitual blue alice band but was hanging loosely around her face. I had never really noticed her lips before but now a vermillion lipstick showed off how full they were. I took one look and thought she had been drinking.

This thought did not stop me inviting her in and offering her a drink - the usual shiraz. Normally Sally would sit on the chair opposite me while I sat on my red leather sofa, but when I came in with the drinks she was seated, leaning back on the sofa, legs apart. I quickly averted my eyes and sat on the chair opposite her. By now my brain had got the message and I was troubled. I liked Sally, liked her a lot, but there was absolutely no place for any sexual dimension in our relationship. We didn't say a word; Sally just stared, smiling, at me, and I looked down and sipped my wine. She patted the red cushion invitingly.

"Come and sit next to me."

"I really don't think I'd better."

She reached inside her bra and pulled out a condom and raised a quizzical, inviting eye. I shook my head, but already aware of a certain arousal and fearing the direction of this interchange.

Then, almost before I had time to register what was happening, Sally was on her knees before me, undoing my belt and pulling down my trousers and pants. Like a masturbating veteran her hands skilfully worked on my penis, but could not get it beyond semi-arousal. I was perplexed. Half of me did not want this to be happening, but the other half wanted to surrender to Sally and give her the fucking she was clearly desperate for. It was the turn of her lips and, again; she so knew what she was doing. Normally I would have sat back and enjoyed it, but in fact I leaned forward and watched those vivid, full lips at work. Normally I might have taken hold of her head and actively forced my penis backwards and forwards in her mouth. But this was not normal – and, hard as Sally tried, I could not get a full erection. This had never happened to me before and I felt a failure. Looking back I can see there was a massive conflict going on between the counsellor and the sexual male. I would have expected the latter to have won out, but on this occasion it didn't. In retrospect that was all for the best. At the time, though, I felt I had failed a masculinity test.

As for Sally she pretended it didn't matter, but she quickly finished off her glass of wine and left. She had offered herself and been turned down: she must have felt rejected and perhaps humiliated. Maybe she blamed the fiasco on my inadequacies. I don't know, but I too felt humiliated, and after I had thought through what might have happened and masturbated gloriously. That evening I resolved to demonstrate to Sally that I was not impotent. I couldn't go around, letting her think that and maybe laughing behind my back. And it was three days before I washed my penis clean of her lipstick.

We met again, just the two of us, twice after that evening. One dark and barmy evening we went for a walk. Initially we behaved as though nothing different had happened between us but, always in the back of my mind,

I was determined to fuck her: I had to reassert my manhood. With this in mind I waited till we had arrived in an alley way just to the side of her house. I pushed her against the fence and pushed myself against her. I had taken her unawares and I soon had my hand under her skirt and was pulling down her panties. She pushed me away forcibly. I persisted for a while, but she was not having any of it.

"Not here, not now." It was outside her daughter's bedroom, and I admit that a part of me wanted to hear Sally come and for her daughter to hear her mother being fucked like a common alley cat. Of course I am ashamed of that thought, but that Saturday evening had dynamited our previous platonic relationship. Sally was no longer simply a good friend in need but also a whore who wanted me.

Sally came round to my house three days later. She went straight upstairs and lay on my bed. She let me undress her and then let me fuck her. I think both our scripts led to this conclusion, but it was loveless. Bone against bone, flesh into flesh, that was it. Not a word spoken. When it was over – and only one of us came – Sally got up, dressed silently, and just said "Goodbye" as she went downstairs and through the front door. I lay in my bed, not yet able to digest what had happened. But I was aware that something had been broken.

That was it. We never met face to face again. We moved in the same social circles but we avoided personal contact. I was going to say that Sally seemed to be avoiding me, but, if truth be known, I think I was avoiding her too. Sex had got in the way of friendship. Perhaps at some level Sally had thought she ought to reward me for the hours of unpaid counselling I had given her and we had got close, but that last Saturday evening was so false. It wasn't the real Sally, though my failure was probably the real me – which makes nonsense of a wounded masculinity taking over and my pressing myself on her.

It's a friendship I regret having lost. We had so much in common: Labour Party and CND obviously. But Sally was broad-spirited. Not only did she want to make the world a fairer and a better place, but she was generous in her personal relationships – by which I mean that she was a giving person and people felt better for her acquaintance. And she had a good brain. She had latterly stopped teaching and was using her Masters degree to work as an archivist in the local library.

Buried away amongst books, on her own, Sally was able to shut herself off from the Rosalind murder furore. In truth this did not last long. The alleged lover of the murdered woman was never identified. Jack moved out of the house he had shared with Sally for twenty-five years, but I was unaware of fingers being pointed at him.

He managed to behave as though nothing had happened. Of course people asked him about the murdered teacher, but his mask of concern and ignorance never slipped. He avoided me all the time. Occasionally I thought I caught a glimpse of worry as he looked at me, but more often it was a defiant scorn that met me. He knew Sally had been seeing me, but I never knew how much he knew about what had happened between us.

I did not know any of the handful of teachers who worked with Jack and Rosalind, but they must have known, or at the very least had had suspicions, about the relationship between the two. But clearly nothing had leaked out to the police. Jack's rejection of me has not endeared him to me, but I must acknowledge that the loyalty of his staff does speak loads in his favour. I suspect, though, that going into school each day and being reminded of Rosalind and his suppressed guilt being stirred, eventually proved too much for Jack. Six months after the murder he took early retirement.

For a couple of years he and Sally continued to live apart, but socially did things together. By now their daughter was off to university and both their sons had settled in villages outside Oxford. Playing the family card

Sally and Jack went off together; they bought a house together and settled near their sons. Of course I was not privy to their thinking, but I suspect the family card was partly a veneer to cover the fact that Jack – though probably not fearful of ever being identified as the lover – felt uncomfortable at living a lie. He needed to get away, reinvent himself, shed the guilt. I wish I knew why Sally decided they could live together again and how they worked it out together.

That is something I will never know. I do know that when I bumped into her, alas with Jack, on an anti-Trump demonstration in London some years later, she was no longer the bony woman she had become during the murder ordeal. She had fleshed out a good deal and acknowledged me with a lovely smile that seemed to come from the depths of a contented human being. The smile we shared was a good smile, but that was all.

Sally had always been keen on football, and the one thing I know about her and Jack's later life was their involvement in Forest Green Football Club, the environmental conscious club with its vegan diet for the players, its solar-powered stadium and its organic pitch – not to mention its electric car power points. Football and principles going together. That's just right for Sally, one of the most warm and progressive people it has been my pleasure to get, once upon a time, to know.

DEBBIE

Of course her name was Deborah but that indicates a stateliness and decorum that no way did she possess. She entered my consulting room all of a flurry, bursting with anger and outrage and perplexity. I calmed her down with a Werther's original, on which she choked – and that slowed her stream of words. She told me the situation in which she found herself, and was chastising herself for her gullibility and for being betrayed. I had to explain to her that before we looked at what was undoubtedly the current issue I needed some background. I needed to know as much about her as she was prepared to divulge. She insisted she would conceal nothing (though in my experience we all have something to hide, something we keep to ourselves). And this is what she told me.

She was one of three children, the middle one with both an elder and a younger brother. She had thought it a secure family unit until, when she was fourteen, her father had suddenly walked out on them. Although he had re-entered her life five years ago, there had been no news, apart from Christmas and birthday cards, about him for twenty years. It was at this time that her elder brother, four years older than Debbie, joined the Marines and began to abuse her. He stopped short of full sexual intercourse with her, but she was taught how to pleasure him both by hand and mouth. Of course her brother was away most of the year so in her despair at missing her father and her loneliness she got into the habit of going for walks at weekends with sex-starved boys from the local boarding school where the sexual skills her brother had taught her were much appreciated. This lasted two or three months. It stopped when one day, instead of the usual two boys waiting for her, there were six and they all started pawing her long before they reached their quiet field. There was something sinister and potentially violent about it all. She sensed rape. And she was afraid. She had no intention of losing her virginity until there was love involved. Before they got to the field, while still in a housing estate, she managed to break free and run home. She was not pursued. Subsequently she stayed at home weekends, reading.

Reading was something she had always enjoyed. Her father was into books and it was a pleasure they had shared together. It stood her in good stead at school, where she always prospered in the Arts subjects. This brought her to the attention of the Headteacher – a man called Chris – who made her a prefect in her last year of secondary school and, when she left, made her promise to stay in touch. In fact staying in touch was not at all difficult for, at sixteen, she simply transferred to the Sixth Form College a mile or so away. It was there that she studied for her A levels – English, History, History of Art – and it was there at the age of seventeen that she experienced another devastating loss. Her mother had divorced her father and was now in a relationship with another man, Trevor, and Trevor wanted to emigrate to Australia and take her mother and the children with him. Halfway through her A levels, Debbie was not budging. But her mother and younger brother went with Trevor, leaving Debbie with an Alsatian dog to look after, little money and a one bedroom flat that she could not afford to heat. Toothpaste was deemed an unnecessary luxury item, and there were times when she shared a tin of dog food.

But she survived – with an awful lot of help from her ex-Headteacher Chris. He used her to babysit frequently and made sure that he fed her on those occasions. And he would find time too to talk with her about her studies, as his degree was also in Literature. Debbie lost her anger when she spoke of Chris: he had been nothing but supportive and loving towards her. Yes, it was to him that she had willingly surrendered her virginity – in her freezingly cold bedroom one night after baby-sitting. She had remained friends with Chris through the years, just occasionally having sex. Mainly, though, it was for support she turned to him. He and his wife – about whom Chris had always declared he was never going to leave - had moved away so it was for the most part phone conversations that they had. I wondered why she had not gone to Chris with this issue she was bringing to me, and Debbie explained that it felt too overwhelming for a distant phone call or two, with maybe a wife half listening-in and demanding to know more. Anyway, she had started doing a counselling course and one of the tutors had recommended me – so here she was!

Debbie was very good, very particular, about details. There was an exactitude about her telling me of her sexual experiences which I have not reported. I was also given an at least emotionally graphic account of her sexual experiences at University. She had decided to stay in England and to ignore her mother's pleas to go to Australia. The flat was sold off - the money going to Australia – and Debbie found herself a room in a commune only two miles from where she was studying. She had stayed local, mainly because of Chris. In fact she could count on the fingers of one hand the number of times she saw him those three years when she took her degree in English Literature. There was, though, one man she saw every day. His name was John and he sort of ran the commune. It was a rundown farmhouse and he had organised the commune from the beginning. He it was who interviewed would-be communards and decided who could have a room there. Apart from him the other four communards were female, and it was understood that all commune members had sooner or later to share his bed. Debbie was reluctant to do this, but was assured by her fellow communards that it was not such a big deal and it was best to get it over with. So, reluctantly, she conformed. She told me exactly what took place. "It could have been worse," she concluded.

There were one or two short-lived sexual trysts while at university, but the techniques she had learned from her brother seemed to more than satisfy the men concerned. "I still fundamentally saw myself as chaste, waiting for the right man to give myself to," she explained. And after university she found the right man. She had got herself a job teaching English at the local Technical College. It was not teaching Shakespeare or Ibsen, Dickens or Hardy, as she would have liked. It was simply a lesson or two a week of basic English for those doing technical courses – chefs, plumbers, nurses. Not at all intellectually demanding and her good looks did mean that the chefs and plumbers in particular were more interested in her than in any real learning.

Technical College was, however, where she met Paul. Paul instructed the chefs and his attention was drawn to Debbie by the ribald comments he heard about her from his trainees. Debbie had turned down any number of invitations to go out with a trainee chef, and initially, thinking that Paul was after the same thing as his students, turned him down, But he persisted and she yielded and they found they got on like the proverbial house-on-fire.

Anyway. They married and quite soon she bore him two children, girls. "That's when I was really happy," she told me. "I did a little part-time work, learned a good deal about cooking and eating well, and my girls were an absolute delight – their freedom and innocence was something I marvelled at." It was at this best of all possible times in Debbie's life that her father re-entered it; I thought she was about to explain but then she frowned, and did not go on. She said little about her marriage. I expect like most people the bliss and jouissance of the early heady days soon became conventional domestic contentment. But Debbie did say how happy she had been and she expected that marriage, that relationship with Paul, to go on for ever – certainly she had never envisaged it ending. One day, though, Paul drove his motorbike into the back of a dustcart and was killed outright, immediately. An inquest found that his brakes had completely failed. The girls were eleven and nine respectively. That was three years ago. Debbie's life had to start again.

In fact her life started again – although at the time Debbie did not know it – on the day of Paul's funeral. Her father had suggested that he would be happy to host the post-funeral drinks at this house, it being more spacious and not full of memories. Debbie accepted gratefully, and after the funeral service at the crematorium – "a lovely service, with all Paul's favourite songs" – she booked a taxi to take her and the two girls from the crematorium to her father's. "I thought I would be too upset to drive there, and too drunk to drive on the way back." The taxi driver's name was Martyn, and he agreed to pick them up to take them home afterwards. Debbie described him as middle-aged with long shoulder-length hair, quietly spoken, very kind to both her and her daughters.

He had given her his personal card when he dropped her at home, telling her that there was no need to ring the central booking office of the taxi company. She could get him direct and, as long as he wasn't on an airport run or the equivalent, he would come. Debbie had a car so she didn't envisage using him, but there was always a difficulty with her elder daughter Laura's weekly cricket practice. The cricket clashed with Debbie's evening class in astrology. This friendly taxi man was the solution! So every week he took Laura to and from her cricket practice, and built up a close rapport with her. Laura pronounced him "ever so nice" and persuaded her mother to invite him in for a drink one evening. Laura was certain that her mother would get on with Martyn. And she did get on with him, very well indeed. Martyn was writing a novel and was supporting himself by taxi driving. They had literary interests in common. Martyn never showed Debbie his novel, but Debbie thought nothing of that as novelists can be very guarded about showing anybody a work in progress.

Debbie was surprised how quickly she got over Paul's death. Very soon – three months at the most – Martyn was filling the gap left by Paul, and not only filling it but adding something to it. There was now an excitement in Debbie's life, an excitement that had been lacking for years. They would go out of an evening and see films together, or go to Indian or Chinese restaurants. And before long there was sex. "I looked forward so much to seeing him. If there was a day when he wasn't around I saw it as a wasted day." He used to drop in at odd times, sometimes when Debbie wasn't there, and that didn't matter for he had such a good relationship with the girls. Especially Laura. They stopped eating out so often and instead ordered take-aways so that the girls could share with them – and, of course, he stayed over. It was like a renewed family unit.

Marriage was inevitable. "It was one of the happiest days of my life." All her friends came to the wedding. Laura and Lesley were bridesmaids. Her wedding photos showed her beaming with delight, with a contentedly smiling Martyn beside her. There was only one thing that scarred that day: her father refused to attend. He wouldn't be explicit about the reasons for his refusal. He just said that he couldn't stand Martyn and that he hoped Debbie knew what she was doing "letting than man into your house." He hoped that he was wrong and that Martyn was no longer the person he had been. Again he had refused to elaborate on this gnomic statement, simply restating that he hoped Debbie was right and that he was wrong.

In fact her father was the one who was right. They had had a short honeymoon weekend in Oxford, curtailed because both of them had expressed a wish to get back to the girls. Martyn and Debbie had had a satisfactory sexual relationship but he had never seemed to be fully committed; his mind was elsewhere. Looking back on what she called **that** afternoon, Debbie saw the signs she had previously ignored, ignored because she had not wanted to believe what they were implying. That afternoon? Debbie came home early, and presumably quietly; what she saw in her living room had been imprinted on her mind and would not go away: Martyn with his trousers down, his penis erect and Laura's hand on the penis. Of course she withdrew her hand immediately, and Martyn pulled up his trousers, when Debbie entered the room. There was a long embarrassed silence, broken by Martyn stumbling out an explanation that Laura had expressed an interest in the male organ and he was responding to her curiosity – nothing more. It didn't wash. Much as Debbie wanted to believe that this was the simple truth she couldn't help remembering other occasions when an early morning naked Martyn had apparently by accident bumped into Laura. She remembered, unnoticed by them, seeing Martyn and Laura walking along arm-in-arm, bodies touching, and hearing an unknown man call out "When you've finished with her pass her onto me, please." It made no sense at the time, but at that moment in the living room it made complete sense. She had read about the taxi drivers of Rochdale and Oxford, and here was something similar not only on her own doorstep but inside her own home. She had married a calculating paedophile and brought him home to her two young daughters.

Debbie was stunned and silent all evening. In bed that night, while stroking her, Martyn held to his explanation that what she had witnessed had been a one off. She couldn't believe him. She chose to believe his protestations that he had never laid a hand on Lindsey, but the evidence about the sexual connection between him and Laura would not go away. How long had this been going on? And under her own roof too. How much did Laura know about it all? Martyn had to go, even if it was like closing the stable door after the horse had bolted. She was furious with herself for not reading the signs, for failing in her essential duty of protecting her daughters. She had fallen for this devious calculating paedophile, had been conned left right and centre. He had been plausible and she had fallen for it. Her guilt knew no bounds. After a sleepless night she ordered Martyn out of her house at breakfast the following morning. Laura was tearful and pleaded with her mother. Lindsey was silent.

And so Martyn left, to a small bedsitter where, Debbie assumed, Laura visited him after school. When Debbie hesitantly told her father about it, he too felt guilty. He thought he should have been more explicit about his doubts about Martyn; he had known him as a paedophile in the past but didn't want to deny his daughter her obvious happiness – and maybe Martyn had changed and moved on... That was what he had told himself. Just one of the stories we tell ourselves, as we cling to an optimism without any basis, in order to avoid confrontation. At first angry with her father, Debbie came round to understanding his thinking – and they bonded again.

But Debbie's life was shattered. The man she believed she had loved had betrayed her; her elder daughter was not speaking to her; her younger daughter was silent but clinging. This was the story she told me in our first few sessions together. I was trying to patch her together. She couldn't face the ignominy if she approached Social Services; she couldn't face the publicity if she brought a legal action against Martyn. I was trying to build up her personal strength so she could confront - and to hell with the consequences – what had happened. Her ego, though, had been completely destroyed; she felt that not only could she not trust her own judgment ever again but that all her life had been a failure, a delusion that she was in control. Talking with Chris on the phone had not helped her. Talking with me was going to take a long, slow time for her to rediscover any inner strength. I could hear her confession, but I could not authoritatively announce forgiveness of her sins.

I was settling in for the long haul and nonetheless racking my brains about a solution for Laura – would she come for counselling? Although Laura denied it Debbie was certain that she was still visiting Martyn for solace and sex; certainly she would have nothing to do with her mother and brushed aside all Debbie's attempts at emotional and physical affection. Laura needed rescuing. It seemed to me that there was no other option than to get Social Services involved. Debbie's thinking was that she would be able, eventually, to rescue her own daughter. We had reached a kind of impasse when something like a miracle occurred.

Martyn became ill, not just with any ordinary illness but with Covid. At first it had seemed to be flu and Debbie had found out because she discovered Laura making food and attempting to surreptitiously smuggle it out of the house. It was for Martyn, and she told Debbie of his symptoms – basically he was helpless. That was when Debbie's practicality kicked in: she oversaw the making of food for Martyn and she contacted the Covid hotline. Laura was able to report all his symptoms and soon an ambulance took him to hospital – where, five days later, he died.

It was like Providence had intervened – and Debbie had no more need of me. Laura – and Debbie – mourned and moved on comparatively speedily. Lindsey developed a confident extraversion that had been driven within; Debbie adjusted almost overnight and returned to her dreamworld of romance with Chris; Laura had escaped being trafficked and threw herself into developing her cricketing skills – and she was ferried to and from the cricket club by her mother.

As for me I was grateful that Covid had intervened and relieved me of my dilemma apropos of Laura and the need to protect her.

MEGAN

Megan was sent to me by her friend, also called Megan: that was the first thing she told me. This Megan in front of me was not quite sure why she was here. I asked her for a few suggestions about what was not quite right in her life, and she initially just parroted that Megan had sensed she was unhappy. "And are you?" I asked. "Not much more than usual was her reply. No, that's not right. I'm usually a pretty happy, cheerful person."

We then established that what had quite recently gone wrong in her life was the end of a relationship. She had been going out for a couple of years with a divorced older man. She couldn't believe her luck when he, a writer of some consequence, had expressed an interest in her, but just as she had begun to see the two of them together as compatible equals, it all finished. (I could see what would attract any man to Megan: she had a beautiful smile in a round face surrounded by short blonde hair, and she had a charming blush.) Megan had been with him twice to visit his mother, and she and the mother had got on swimmingly. She and Alex had looked at a bungalow together, which seemed to indicate that they might be going to live together – and then it was all over. Megan herself had ended the relationship when she had discovered that Alex had slept with someone else. Megan's friend Megan had advised her to turn a blind eye to the perceived infidelity – Alex had slept just the once with one of his old girlfriends and friend Megan had admitted to having done the same. Friend Megan had seen it as almost natural and no big deal. But the Megan in front of me was not going to accept what had happened. She had known that her relationship was too good to last; they always were, that was her experience.

Of course I wanted to know about her other experiences, but first of all I wanted to know about the other Megan and their closeness. Megan's face lit up at the opportunity to talk about her friend. They had been friends since their first day together at Primary School. They had gone to different Secondary Schools, but had as teenagers always spent time together and had always holidayed together. The other Megan had married in her early twenties – some fifteen years ago – but their friendship had continued and 'my' Megan was always invited to share the same circle of friends as her friend Megan. She had always gone alone to social gatherings until she met Alex, and then he accompanied her. Alex had, though, apparently found her circle of friends very dull and boring. And he had once only introduced her to his circle of friends, where she had embarrassed herself and everybody else by not being able to pronounce Nietzsche – and then not knowing who he was!

Slowly Megan was beginning to warm to me, but on the first session I judged she was not ready to talk about her relationships. I asked her about any siblings she had and her parents. She had one younger sister Michelle and the two sisters lived together in a two-up two-down terraced house. Michelle had a lover/boyfriend who visited whenever he could, which was whenever he could get away from his wife. This arrangement had been going on for years and Michelle seemed happy enough, realising that Barry was never going to leave his handicapped wife. Megan had been entrusted by her parents to look after Michelle; they saw Megan as the sensible one and Michelle as being vulnerable. "They are always phoning or dropping in to see how we are. We do their shopping and things like that. They are very involved in our lives, wanting to know what is going on – and always asking when one of us is going to give then a grandchild. Well, my mother is, anyway."

I asked if she felt her parents were dependent on her and, after a pause, Megan said she thought they were. There was no need for them to be as, they were healthy enough and only in their middle sixties. Her father, though, was asthmatic and a little frail. He had been a plumber. Every day they had some contact with their parents. "They want to know everything that is going on in our lives." This for the second time.

It was half way through our second session together that Megan took a deep breath and really opened up about her relationships and why she expected to be disappointed by them. This is her history. After 1967, when she was fifteen she used to wear flowers in her hair whenever she could (and, I assured her, I got the San Francisco and Scott McKenzie reference.) She was happy to be called Merry Meg and in her sixth form days quite often went to drug and sex parties at the weekend. But that had just been fun and friendly. It had all gone wrong when, early one evening, she had not felt well and had decided to go home. One of the group she was with offered to walk her home and, as they were leaving he winked at his friends. Halfway home he pushed her into a shop doorway and raped her, and then left her to stagger home alone. What this boy said to his friends she never knew, but from then onwards she was seen as a slut and had to push away, often physically, boys who wanted to have her. One of the main reasons, she explained, for her going to London and joining the Civil Service after her A levels was to get away from her home district and her reputation. I resisted at this stage asking what had brought her back home. She had started, almost full pelt, about her sex life and needed to get it all out and over with.

She then told me about a holiday she and Megan had taken together to Tunisia when they were twenty one. It had been just lying around in the sun and reading. They two had been by far the youngest visitors and had got chatting and friendly with a couple of the waiters at the hotel. The night before they were due to return home the waiters had invited them back to their house for a farewell drink. Why not? And they had climbed on the back of mopeds, all excited, and been driven the couple of miles to a little ground floor apartment the waiters shared. All seemed fine and friendly and they were being plied with plenty of alcohol until they realised that more and more young men had entered the apartment and it was unmistakeable what they all had in mind for the Megans. "We had to get out and the door was blocked." They had shared panic-stricken looks and gone to the loo, where, they had found an open window, climbed out and escaped, running all the way, back to their hotel. It had been a lucky escape.

Megan had chosen to tell me about two difficult and painful experiences. Clearly those dominated her past. There must have been other, better experiences, though: she was an attractive woman, surely someone must have loved her and treated her well. I put this to her, and at first she shook her head. "I got to be choosy who I had sex with. And I don't think anyone thought of me as a long term prospect, as it were." She paused. "Not at that time anyway, But later, nearly fifteen years later there was Michael." By this time Megan was working as a PA to the local branch of an electricity company. The works' Christmas party saw the beginning of her affair with Michael. It had begun so sillily. Accidentally some apple sauce had been spilt down the back of Megan's dress. She went to the cloakroom to wash it off and Michael accompanied her. She took off her blouse to wash her back, Michael helped by taking off her bra, and that triggered off a sexual explosion; she put her arms round his neck, he thrust her to the wall and they fucked. They were met with cheers when they returned to the dining table and Megan had blushed to the very core of her being. That was the beginning of her affair with Michael. He was an outside engineer, but came into the office from time to time. It helped that their Christmas Party fling had been observed for, whenever Michael did come into the office, somehow time was made for them to be together.

I asked Megan if she thought she was being used, but she was adamant that this was not so. "He was a nice guy. He treated me well." Apparently he even had managed to fit in a visit to her at home, and once, she and her sister had been being fucked simultaneously in different rooms. Megan smiled at the thought. I asked her why Michael did not visit more often, fearing that I already knew the answer – and I was right: he was a married man with children.

I wondered whether either she or Michelle ever mentioned – or indeed introduced – their lovers to their parents. No way had there been, nor would there be such an introduction. And the once that Michelle had mentioned Barry en passant she had been subjected to a moral inquisition from her mother that had precluded any further mention of the subject. Megan and Michelle's mother still imposed her standards on her daughters, doubtless claiming it was motivated by love and their own best interests.

What had happened to Michael? Eighteen months after their apple sauce induced fling, he had emigrated with his family to Australia. "I don't think they knew about me. It was just an excellent opportunity for him. It was always going to end. They always do." But she still annually receives a Christmas card from him.

There seemed to me two areas to examine further: her treatment by men and her mother. While I pondered on where to lead Megan next I asked her about her sister. Michelle was four years younger than Megan. She hadn't studied for A levels; she was more outdoors and sporty. She still played badminton – that was her social event of the week. And she worked selling clothes in a department store. Apart from her badminton evening, once she was home from work, she stayed at home, slumped in front of the television, watching soaps with her sister, waiting for a phone call from Barry. She cooked occasionally, but it was Megan who organised what they were going to eat and organised the food shopping. Their mother phoned every evening to make sure they were all right. When I suggested that they seemed to be infantilising Michelle, Megan's response was that Michelle **was** the baby of the family and she needed protecting. When I asked from what she needed protection Megan merely shrugged her shoulders. Was there something very wrong with Michelle that I was not being told? Megan was adamant that there was not: she simply was the youngest and so, on behalf of her family, she had to look after her. That was why when her mother decreed that the two girls should live together – and made a financial offer "which they could hardly afford" as a deposit on a house – there was no way Megan could refuse.

I wanted too to know about her stay after her A levels in London. I had assumed that she had stayed there for years, avoiding coming back to the place where she had an unwanted (and unjustified) sexual reputation. But no, she had lived there barely a year. "I was living in a hostel alone, I barely knew anybody. I felt a bit like a country bumpkin. I was miserable." There was also the factor that absence left a hole in the family home: she was missed and her mother hated to see her miserable and assured her that she would be far happier back home. So, after ensuring that she had a secretarial job forty minutes' travelling distance from her home town, Megan returned. And she had been delighted that, although she rarely had gone out, her 'reputation' seemed to have been forgotten. She had returned home just before Christmas, "And it was lovely. My mother always spoils us something rotten over Christmas."

I was going to have to tackle the infantilising, dependent mother soon. But I just wanted clarification of Megan and her attitude to relationships with men. Now that her relationship with Alex was over and **she** had ended it, was she looking for another relationship? "I suppose if one comes along, I wouldn't say no. But I'm not actively looking for one." I asked her what she wanted from a relationship and she referenced her friend Megan, who had an undemanding, reliable and kind partner – and one child to whom my Megan was godmother. Megan just wanted to be warm and secure and loved – "like it is in a family". She was not averse to having a child but didn't want to be in a relationship where her looks and available sexuality were the most important things to her partner. She wanted a man to be kind to her.

That was when I asked Megan to give me an example of someone who had been kind to her sometime in her life. She immediately responded with her friend Megan, and then I waited while she paused for quite a long time. "I suppose Alex was kind," she eventually came out with. There had been no mention of her parents so I challenged her about this. And then she began to explore what was becoming increasingly obvious to me: that her parents were not only exploiting their children but infantilising them. Megan didn't use those words; initially she acknowledged that they had become a burden, in so far as they expected their shopping to be done for them and for their daughters to be at all times available. "We don't get much breathing space."

I said it felt to me that "her parents …" – I was corrected: "my mother" – constantly puts pressure on her and Michelle to conform to their template as to how daughters 'should' behave. Megan agreed. There was constant pressure. As long as she fulfilled the role assigned to her she was their dutiful and appreciated daughter, but any spark of – possibly wayward – individuality would most likely be met with disapproval. "I am constantly trying to please my mother," Megan admitted. She realised what she had said and where these thoughts were leading her: it wasn't just the horrendous sexual experiences that had destroyed her self-confidence, it was also her being bullied into meeting the demands of her mother, demands she was never going to fulfil. She still lived within a mile of her parents; it was a long umbilical cord.

Family is a place of love, not duty, we agreed. We worked together on various ideas for separating from her mother. I thought there was a strong case for making a clean break until her mother recognised the individuality and the individual needs of Megan, but Megan thought that would be too cruel. What we came up with was to leave the phone off the hook most evenings, to delay in getting shopping, to occasionally challenge her mother's views. It didn't feel like strong enough tactics to me, and I wasn't sure that Megan would have the determination to carry them out. She said she would give it a try and she would, of course, enlist the support of Michelle. She left, agreeing to return in three months to report back on how her campaign for liberty was progressing.

She never did return. I suspect that she had neither the energy nor the strength to challenge her mother in any way. I'm sure she tried, but she was stuck in a role which had been determined for her long ago. Her friend Megan was right to suggest she needed counselling, but the low level of disappointment with her life almost certainly continued.

I live in a small town, so I am aware of some subsequent developments. Both Megan's parents developed illnesses not long after our counselling sessions – which, I am sure, meant their having an even greater dependency on their daughters. It was not the ideal time for Megan to make any kind of break from them. But these were serious illnesses and in the course of two or three years they both died. And out of their deaths came something positive: the daughters inherited a house (which they sold) and some savings and were able to achieve a measure of independence. They now no longer live together; each has a house of her own and they don't see each other that often. I really have no idea about subsequent forays into relationships, but I do espy Megan from time to time as she walks a black poodle through the town.

She was a very attractive woman, with a decent brain and a desperate yearning for love and kindness. I think when she came to me she was set in the mould of a subservient daughter, a role out of which she was unlikely to break. So much potential, so unfulfilled. Families can be the most oppressive tyrants of all.

PAULA

Paula was short, less than five foot. There was a time when she had been in a relationship with a man who suffered from dwarfism and was even shorter than she was. Waddling along the road together they had looked like two characters from Mary Norton's novel *The Borrowers*. That relationship had not lasted long – hardly troubled the scorer as we say in cricket parlance – but then she had gone to the other extreme. She was now dwarfed by a six foot six giant of a man and indeed had married him. His name was Paul and I liked him, but my friend Paula was always in his shadow. And not just because of his height. His whole being demanded attention. He needed to be the life and soul of the party and Paula, by his side, was almost an incidental, an adjunct.

I knew Paula well. She was a fellow counsellor and on an informal basis we supervised each other, that is we checked out how we were handling our respective clients. She could be very insightful and helpful. In the past we had occasionally co-counselled together, listening to the other's issues and facilitating some kind of acceptance or resolution. This time, though, there was no question of sharing each other's issues. There would be nothing reciprocal. Paula needed to talk, to explore, and she would pay me for it.

I didn't need to do what I call 'the usual background check' with Paula. I knew so much of her early life and relationships and experiences that we could focus almost immediately on the issue that was troubling her – her family relationships and her need for recognition and to be noticed. Before we go there, though, I need to fill in what I already knew about Paula before that first professional session.

She had been born in Putney just after the War. Her father had returned from having spent months in a

Japanese prisoner-of-war camp and Paula was the result of his sexual celebration with his wife on his return. She acquired a younger brother two years' later, but whereas Paula was always afraid of her father and was a little goody-two-shoes at home, her brother was always in trouble and always experiencing the wrath and belt of their father. Her mother was a quiet, uncomplaining woman who just got on with things and kept the household running smoothly. She wasn't one for cuddles but what affection Paula experienced was always from her mother. Her father's contribution was to hold down a regular job as a bookkeeper and so finance their little household.

At school Paula was clever enough in a quiet, industrious way. She just got on with things without receiving much notice or attention. Short with short straight hair, in no ways at all did she stand out from the crowd. It was only in her mid-teens that she realised that she possessed something that the male of the species was after and that gave her a certain power that she had hitherto not felt. She mainly exercised this power at the Youth Club that she and her brother Jasper attended twice a week. After a bit of table tennis and chat with the girls Paula spent a lot of the evening flirting with boys. "I knew what they wanted, but they never got it all. I made them happy, though – it wasn't difficult!"

While Paula was giving satisfaction to her adolescent male friends, her brother was wheeling and dealing. He always had some scam or scheme going on which brought him money. Their father despaired of him and frequently threatened to disown him. Had he been alive when Jasper was given his first jail sentence that would doubtless have happened, but he died when Paula was sixteen and Jasper fourteen. "Worn out by the War, probably." That was when Jasper had gone completely out of control and his life had been subsequently one dodgy venture after another. He had been sent to young people's prison institutions, but their impact on him was minimal. Paula never had had any time or feeling of closeness for Jasper –

"a minor irritant who became a major irritant." Once Paula left home she hardly ever saw him again. She knew he was in and out of jail, that he had fathered two sons. That was about it. When she heard, in her fifties, that he had died in a Spanish jail, that was the first she had known of him for more than a decade. That kind of death was inevitable; Paula felt she had seen it coming since they were children, and she did not grieve. But she did dutifully maintain contact with Jasper's two children and then their children.

Paula left home at the age of seventeen. She couldn't get away quickly enough. Home had never been a place of ease or comfort or love and, since the death of her father, it had become a place of meanness and frugality – and even more tension. She enrolled on a secretarial course and found a cheap bedsit in Crouch End. Her finances were low and at weekends she would go into town and hang around bars until someone picked her up and took her out for a meal. At times she ate well – but there were always afters, usually quick and uncomfortable down a dark alley. On one such Saturday night foray into town Paula picked up a soldier. He wasn't particularly good looking but he was short like Paula. They had a couple of drinks before they set off for the Indian meal that Paula had negotiated in return for sex and they hit it off. Mainly flirting and sex talk. "He was my age. We were young and free and foolish."

They lingered over the Indian meal – "my first chicken biryani; I've loved them ever since." And then they lingered over the sex; it was not poor, nasty, brutish and short as it usually was. Nor did Paula feel solitary; they were in it together and, for once, she was not merely being used. When it was over they had another drink and then went dancing. "We were high and hit it off. He was called Derek and he was off to Singapore with his army regiment in a month's time. I said I would miss him and he said 'why not come with me?'" Excitedly, Paula accepted the invitation, but it meant that they had to get married so that married quarters would be available in Singapore. And indeed they got married in a fever. The secretarial training was abandoned and off they flew to Singapore.

It was all fine and dandy at first. "Though I never got used to the heat." Their married quarters were a flat in a compound surrounded by other army couples. There was a communal swimming pool. That was where Paula spent most of her time, lounging around the pool with other housewives. The Officers had their club for wives, the other ranks (which, of course, included Derek) had a swimming pool. Derek was off on manoeuvres or training most of the time, so Paula had time on her hands. All she was required to do was a minimal amount of housework, cook Derek an evening meal and sleep and have sex with him. She had time on her hands and read a lot. At first it was just magazines, which was what most of her fellow housewives were reading. "Quite frankly, we were all bored. We could have done with Gareth Malone."

Paula began to read contemporary novels: she remembered *The Outsiders, Rosemary's Baby, Picnic at Hanging Rock* and *Nicholas and Alexander.* This latter novel by Robert K Massie had got her into an interest in historical novels which she had maintained to this day. At first it was Jean Plaidy, then Alison Weir, then Philippa Gregory. The Tudors have become her go-to comfort area. She loves C J Sansom's Shardlake novels but confesses to having a block with regard to Hilary Mantel. I digress – though perhaps someone's comfort reading does reveal something about them. In this case? Retreat into a safe known world? I actually think that reading *Rosemary's Baby* and *The Outsiders* at this early time of her life tells us much more.

She was bored. The excitement had gone. And she was pregnant. Her once exciting husband could think only of food and sex. Neither Paula nor the forthcoming baby seemed to interest him. For the most part Paula lived in an all female gated community. There was no opportunity for an affair to enliven her life. The man who cleaned the swimming pool was ancient and, even if he had been available, Paula did not rate her pulling appeal in comparison with what she saw as so many better looking women.

The birth – James – was no problem, and she stuck it out there for another year, before she announced that she had had enough, both of Derek and Singapore. She and James were leaving. Back she came to England, divorced (there was no opposition from Derek) and set about earning a living. It was in the days when Council flats were available, before Thatcher ruined the whole system. With what I would call a fair amount of characteristic vigour and determination, Paula set to work to make a living which would support herself and James. This initially involved regular evening bar work. The pub was just down the road and Paula established herself as a popular, regular fixture. It was through her work that she met her second husband Melvyn. He had his own two man building company and instead of coming into the bar for an occasional drink he began to come in every night. He was a shy, quiet man. After a couple of months he got round to asking Paula out for a date and a month later he asked her to marry him. "I couldn't have been happier."

For Paula those ten years of being married to Melvyn were the happiest of her life. They bought a house together and she had two more children, both boys – Danny and Wayne. "Melvyn's choice of names." Melvyn was kind and reliable and let Paula make most of their decisions. "I felt important." She still did some bar work, but she had a new career interest: Playschools. It began when she took James to his playgroup; she began to help out there and liked it so much that she enrolled for a Playgroup leader course and then became a Playgroup leader and consultant. "I was happy. I was someone."

All good, and then, out of the blue, Melvyn died. He was forty-five. Paula woke up one spring morning and went to wake the man by her side, but there was no response. He had died peacefully in his sleep, a weak heart was diagnosed. His children were ten and eight. Complete devastation. Apart from the psychological and emotional damage that Melvyn's death caused, there was a financial catastrophe. Paula's playgroup work was mainly honorary so she was driven to train for a career that would be financially rewarding, and that is when she chose counselling! "For two years I put the future before the present, if you see what I mean. I trained and did more bar work in the evenings. It was a financial necessity. But the boys had lost their dad and, I think, felt that they were also losing their mother. I certainly did not give them enough time - or love. James was away at College by then and I certainly was not concerned about him. And he had not lost a father. But I *had* lost a husband. I think I hid my grief and buried myself in work and training. It was not a good time."

Paula had told me all that a few years ago, but I am pretty sure that I have accurately recalled what she said. There followed years of just about getting by, but into his teens Danny began to go off the rails bigtime. Little mean acts of bullying younger boys, writing obscenities on toilet walls, and then staying out to all hours, mainly drinking but with some drug taking. When he was seventeen he was sent to Feltham Young Offender Institution for stealing a car and driving under the influence of drink and with no licence or insurance. That experience of prison had such an impact on Danny that he had been deterred from pursuing any more criminal activities, but he had drifted along from one bedsit to another, not quite down and out but increasingly reliant on alcohol. He had been out of control for years and had fruitlessly occupied enormous chunks of Paula's time. Wayne, by her own admission, had consequently been neglected by Paula. He was no problem, just quietly getting on with his life and being horrified by the behaviour of his elder brother.

That pattern of behaviour has continued through the years: James being distant; Danny being a problem, mainly with drink, and Wayne keeping to himself. Paula had thought that it would all improve as the boys matured and especially when James and Danny married – Wayne remaining resolutely single. And to an extent it had, especially with Danny and his Thai bride; Danny still drank a lot but he did hold down various menial jobs. From time to time Danny needed 'loans' from his mother, but apart from that, the weight of responsible motherhood had been removed from Paula's shoulders. James had married a woman some fifteen years older than he was but had a secure life in IT, and Wayne was working for Shell petroleum in Malaysia, rarely returning to the UK.

It was the heartache she experienced from the lack of closeness to her sons that was dragging Paula down. James lived a mere five miles away but she saw him only at Christmas. There had been times when he was working in Denmark and she could tell herself that he was not available for most of the year, but now she could no longer deceive herself. He was deliberately keeping his distance. She knew that she and James's wife did not get on, but she felt that James could have made more of an independent effort to see his mother. She was clearly no more of use to him, and she felt her only use to Danny was as an alternative bank. With regards to Wayne he was always superficially pleasant on the rare occasions they met, but Paula felt that he went through the expected rituals of filial duty but always kept himself to himself.

That was what Paula fundamentally wanted to share with me. "I brought these boys up single-handed for most of their lives. And they keep me at a distance. My friends talk to me about their closeness to their children and their delight in their grandchildren. I get nothing from my children." Paula was at pains to express that she wasn't one of those sentimental women who needed grandchildren to drool over. Grandchildren were not the point: receiving love and recognition from her children was.

Paula's feelings of dissatisfaction and rejection were exacerbated by seeing at close hand how loving were the relationships between her husband Paul and his son and daughters. There were what felt like non-stop two way visits and hugs. His children were middle-class successful and his grandchildren, four in all, were warm and friendly and seemed to be happy and balanced. Paula had tried to discuss this difference between the two sets of children with Paul, hoping for some understanding, and he had initially simply luxuriated in how wonderful his children were and how that must reflect on his parenting skills before going on to criticise the way Paula must have brought up her children. This was not what she had wanted to hear. She just wanted her heartache to be heard and acknowledged. Which is why she had now come to me.

All I could do was listen. It was fruitless for me to point out that she might have emotionally neglected her children in the quest to put food on the table. – something that so many parents do, especially in these times of austerity. She knew that. It was equally pointless for me to point out that I have clients who bemoan a lack of children on the, obviously false, assumption that children automatically bring happiness and purpose to one's life. What I could do, though, was to ask her about her relationship with Paul. I thought that might lead us somewhere that would shed light on Paula's behaviour patterns.

She began by saying how content she was and, apart from Melvyn, this was the best relationship she had been in. "But?" I queried. She paused, and then told me that the worst thing was to be financially dependent on Paul. Paul didn't abuse this, but this feeling of being less worth just underlay everything. "Somehow he's always in the driving seat." And she added that, as a couple, the attention was always on Paul and she was almost invisible by his side as an adjunct. She warmed to this theme, explaining that similarly when she was with her dwarf partner he had always wanted to be the life and soul of the party, had always demanded attention and she had been, in company, pretty well ignored. "It's a pattern I don't like. I have been subservient for too long. Perhaps I don't need love, perhaps I don't need appreciation – though that would be nice. I just want to be noticed. To be at the centre of my own life. I've spent too long serving others- even in my professional life! Somehow I need to find the strength to say 'This is me!' and for people to sit up and take notice."

We had got to the core of Paula's problems. Living and caring for others had produced no rewards, was unsatisfactory. She knew that as early as her Singapore days when her life had been limited to providing food and sex. She had escaped, but had always subsequently been forced into a life of servitude because of her lack of financial independence. At last she had acknowledged her own need to project herself positively. Quite how to do something about this was the problem. That was what we together would be working on for the next few weeks.

REBECCA

My History of Art class contained some interesting people: there was the lovely elderly Jewish man Harry, there was the retired librarian Alex and there was Rachel, a dark haired socialist whom I secretly fancied. All of these I liked; I felt ease with them. Then there was, amongst seven or eight others, Rebecca. She made sure you noticed her. She would invariably arrive late for class, making an impression as she swept in, her ankle-length skirt moving gracefully as she did. Her perfume lingered. She had a posh voice too. Most people adjust their voice to the company they are keeping at the time – she didn't. She was tall with short semi-curly black hair, rosey cheeks too. She was outspoken in her responses to the paintings we discussed: I remember her scorn of most of the Pre-Raphaelite and her fascination with Hieronymus Bosch's triptych *The Garden of Delights.* I saw her as a confident well-spoken, attractive woman, but I was more interested in Rachel and, I suppose also that a part of me thought that Rebecca was out of my league.

So imagine my surprise when, at the end of one class, she approached me for a confidential word. She knew that I worked as a counsellor and she had something she needed to talk about – would I see her, soon? Of course I said yes, and, at her insistence, she came to see me at five in the evening the next day – a dark November evening. I was tired, wanting to leave my counselling room and drive home when she arrived, but she soon had me interested, if not quite enchanted. Sex and relationships were what she wanted to talk about. She jumped straight in to tell me so, though admittedly blushing very fetchingly as she did so. Her husband of fifteen years wanted an open relationship; basically she was happy about that, and he had already begun to see other women. But this meant that her sexual needs were not being met; she wanted to discuss her options with me.

Fair enough, but I explained that I wanted to know more about her – that a sex drive was only a part of our identity, and she laughed at that. What I learned was that she had been born into a professional family in the Midlands and that she was the middle of three sisters: her elder sister was a successful lawyer, married to an American and living in Los Angeles and her younger sister was an unsuccessful writer with big dreams and little money. She herself was, with her husband, the joint Head of a small independent boys' school, a Prep School. He in fact was the nominal Head, but they saw it as a joint enterprise – and incidentally, she added, they intended their educational work together to continue however their relationship issues were resolved. That was the cue for her to say how much happier her husband now seemed as he was dating other women, and how she was becoming envious and therefore wanted my guidance.

She was grateful to her husband, Alexander, for having rescued her, but that was a long time ago, and she recognised their marriage had run its course – but their three children, two boys and a girl, all in their teens, needed them to stay together to give them the security of a happy family. "It might be an illusion but it's better than my childhood. My father was a bully and my mother suffered – so did we all." I made the assumption that Alexander had rescued her from the malign influence of her father, but she quickly put me right. It was from her students. She explained. "When I was at university I was what you might call a bit of a wild girl. I had escaped from an oppressive family – my father, as I have said, was a bully – and I let my hair down. Simple as that. But I've always had good energy levels, so I could both party and study. I had lots of boyfriends. I enjoyed sex. And I got a first class degree and stayed on to do an MA. While I was working on my MA I got work as a part-time tutor. That's when things began to get out of hand. I thought I was simply popular amongst my young male students, but apparently I got a reputation as an easy lay." She grimaced. "Anyway. Alex, who was a lecturer in a different Department from mine but whom I knew reasonably well, overheard my students talking about me in a bar one night. About what, collectively, they would like to do to me: invite me to a party, get me drunk and then 'fuck me silly' was apparently the expression that was used. They had already drawn lots as to who was to have me first and they were in the process of imaging graphically all the different things they were going to do to me when Alex left. It could just have been student talk and bravado but Alex was genuinely concerned and told me. I'm so glad he did for I hardly ever could resist an invitation to a party. Almost overnight I sobered up. I took stock, anyway. Alex offered to help – which meant that in the first place I went out with him only and we were seen together as an item. At first it was an act but in time we grew closer. We married and I have been faithful ever since. I was the first woman Alex ever was fully intimate with, but he was a good learner. Now, though, he has a similar urge to the one I had twenty years ago and he is eager for new experiences. And I'm here, unsure about where to go next."

Rebecca was very confident in talking about herself. She knew she was attractive to men – that was not a problem. What she was fearful of was that she might be tempted to return to the days of her youth and thus "lose all my self-respect."

All this came out in our first two sessions, mainly in the second one. There was more stuff about her relationships with her sisters and her academically successful school days. Stuff too about high jumping and the book she had written on market research. Also about her and Alexander working together, how they distributed their responsibilities equally. There was a good deal too about her "lovely" children and when I questioned her about the ethics of working in the education private sector, she vehemently said that she felt, as a Conservative, no need to defend what she was doing.

I haven't got any more details about the other aspects of her life mentioned in the previous paragraph, for it was the sexual aspect of her life that was most concerning her and with which I was entrusted to help her move on. I must confess that, as the evening got darker and darker outside my consulting room, I fought off becoming aroused by the stories I heard. (She elaborated on her time as a student, though I have chosen not to write about any of it.) Here was I alone with a beautiful, trusting, sexually frustrated woman. I had to stop my mind racing and fantasising; I had to remain professional.

Our third session together was where it all went wrong – or right, depending on your perspective. Rebecca lived a mere half mile from me. She suggested it was silly us both driving twenty miles for our sessions. Why didn't I see her at my house? No one else had ever suggested this, though it obviously made sense. I concurred and made my living room as impersonal as possible – taking down my family photos. At seven o'clock – both of us having finished our usual working day – Rebecca arrived. She did blush quite easily, but that evening she was blushing as she entered the door. And then she asked me to put the champagne bottle she had brought in the fridge. "I thought we might like to drink it when we have finished." I put it in the fridge and sort of realised what was going on. I didn't resist. I motioned to my red leather settee for Gabrielle to sit and I drew up a chair opposite her. We had hardly begun when she raised her eyebrows challengingly and patted the seat next to her. I accepted the invitation and immediately we were all over each other. Clothes came off easily – she (always) wore nothing beneath her voluminous skirt – and soon we were stroking each other all over and moaning with delight. I put her on her back and was preparing to enter her when she stopped us. She was panting with longing (as was I) but suddenly her brain took over. "I want this as much as you do," she said, "but we must have an HIV test first, both of us." I demurred, saying that I was pretty certain that I was 'safe', and she said she was certain she was too, but, for her, it was important to be sure. It is true too that it was a time when HIV was top of people's medical concerns. So the rest of the evening we sat on my couch, semi-naked, kissing, touching, stroking – and drinking champagne.

It was ten days before the AIDS test results came back for both of us. In the meantime we spoke on the phone and talked sex. Rebecca's imagination knew no bounds: from cross-dressing to bondage to anal she wanted it all. So when both our tests came back negative, as we were pretty sure they would, we began our sexual feasts and indulgence. I think it was liberating for us both. Sometimes Rebecca would send me a script in advance indicating what scenario she wanted playing out. At other times, with no script, we would improvise there and then. Sexually there were no dull moments. She was a brown-eyed girl, with delightful rosebud breasts and strong haunches and a slightly rounded belly. Full of passion and energy. We came together at what seems to have been the right time for both of us. I guess we exploited each other but they were good, if exhausting, times.

Most of the time was spent at my house and in my bed – indeed Rebecca's complaints about the uncomfortable nature of my mattress led to my buying a new one. (I also purchased a headboard to which we could tie each other.) Only once did I spend a night at Rebecca's house: that was when her husband and children were away for, perforce, I had to be her clandestine lover. She was very concerned that her adolescent children were not disturbed by their mother having a lover. Which all meant that we rarely went out in public together. If we did it was in the larger town twenty miles away. We went once – disastrously, for it was a vampire movie and I was almost sick and we had to leave early – to the cinema and I think we had two Sunday lunches together, always looking over our shoulders to check we had not been recognised. Rebecca ate well and the one night I spent in her bed she had so filled me with food that I was more inclined to sleep than be sexually active.

Meat, fruit and vegetables, all good for energy, was Rebecca's staple diet. And bread – she was a mean bread maker. Sex was her main way of using her energy. She had a dog, a Border Collie, which she took for walks, but that did not use up that much energy. Once upon a time, not long before we met, she had used to go running in the early morning, wearing a very short pair of tight white shorts. On one such run she had been sexually accosted – she refused to tell me what exactly had happened – and that had put paid to that form of exercise.

So sex it was, and she had chosen me. Provided we met a couple of times a week – and as we were both working that was probably the average – everything was fine. I could meet Rebecca's demands. Somewhere I have a letter from her saying what a wonderful lover I was, and then there were times when she would flounce off as I had not met all her needs. She was nothing if not volatile – and, I might add, capricious. You never knew exactly where you were with Rebecca; she controlled the emotional landscape. I was going to add to that "except when she was submissively tied down", but that was always a scenario that came from her so in a way she even controlled that. I once made the mistake of saying to her that if I hadn't had sex for five days my body told me that it needed it. She chose to interpret my comment as my wanting sex only every five days. I did not mean that, but that is how she chose to see it – and she threw a tantrum and lambasted me for being a lousy lover and walked out. She was very proud and could do anger infinitely better then I could. It was a tumultuous topsy-turvy relationship. But it lasted for nearly four years – and she always came back.

Not going out together, not doing anything much except sex, was (is) not normal. We did, though, have a week in Ireland together, a week which brought to a head one of the main differences between us. That was sexual needs, in fact – perhaps sexual capacity.

I had been to Ireland for the first time two years earlier, and I loved the country. Now Rebecca and I attempted to repeat my experience. We flew there and hired a car and drove round from one bed and breakfast to another, with me doing, by agreement, all the driving. There were some good memories – the wonderful bleakness of Connemara and Yeats's tower in Sligo for example – but overall I am still haunted by the almost perpetual tension between us. Rebecca had to have at least one ice cream a day and it had to be a Walls ice cream, a white Magnum or nothing. And, try as we could and did, we could not find a Walls outlet – and this failure somehow became my fault. It was only on the third day that we discovered that Walls traded by a different name (Heartbrand) in Ireland. Nowadays I (and I suspect Rebecca) can laugh at that, but, trivial as it may seem, in those days it was no laughing matter, and somehow mirrored in Rebecca's mind my sexual inadequacies. I just wasn't reliable.

Sexually it was fine for the first three days. The rot set in in Killarney. Rebecca had a scenario that she wanted to enact. She was to dress – all suspender belt etc. – as a whore, and I was to treat her as such and sex would become a financial transaction. Unfortunately we did not have an en suite room; the bathroom/changing room was twenty or so yards down the corridor. I lay in bed while she went to the bathroom to dress appropriately. While she was transforming herself into a tart two new male arrivals started talking to the landlady in the corridor between the bathroom and our room. She waited and waited – and so did I. By the time the corridor was clear – some half an hour later – I had dozed off and she was angry. We exchanged sleepy and angry words, and she threatened to go and offer herself to the two men who had talked so much. So, unsatisfactorily, we went through the motions. And then in Dublin on our last night she decided that she would sleep alone, in a separate room.

Once back home we reverted to meeting perhaps twice a week, and for a while we almost returned to genuinely pleasuring each other, but beneath it was a rumbling dissatisfaction. She still walked out on me occasionally, and still always came back – but the peace between us was always uneasy. Rebecca was considerably wealthier than I was and I was constantly aware of this financial inbalance between us. What brought our relationship to a conclusion, however, was when she decided to move house and she asked me to accompany her in her viewing of two houses and to give my opinion thereon. She was infinitely more into architecture and design than I was, and all I could find to say about the houses was bland and insubstantial. She wanted an opinion from me on a subject about which my opinions were not worth having. Once again I had disappointed her. That was it really. Three weeks later she ended our relationship – amicably. And she had a new project: I was in the past and she was reshaping her life with a new house to design as nearly as possible as she wanted it.

I have no idea whether that marked the end of Rebecca's days of sex and fun. In fact I know very little now about her. In the intervening years I have bumped into her a couple of times and she has been very amicable and blushed to the roots of her being, which was not only appropriate but, for me, still very attractive. For a while she used to work at the university as a student counsellor, with special reference to sexual issues. No comment – other than I have at this juncture to curb my imagination!

It must be seven or eight years since I have heard anything about her. I used to send her birthday greetings but these elicited no response. Last year I bumped into her younger sister and arranged to have coffee with her, my motive being to find out how Rebecca was and what was happening in her life. When I asked her sister she simply said how impossible and patronising she had always found Rebecca and they had not spoken for six years. She had nothing she could tell me. Which was disappointing – I would love to know where all that energy is now going.

I suppose you could say that Rebecca kept me on my toes for all those years together. For me it was an experience that is firmly etched in my mind. She saw herself as somewhat superior and she had the self-confidence that appears to come easily to a beautiful and graceful – and Tory – woman. Beneath the sophistication, though, there was a raw, wild energy. I was privileged to see both sides of her. She was a remarkable woman.

Milton Keynes UK
Ingram Content Group UK Ltd.
UKHW010018030424
440481UK00001B/11